THERE ARE TWO KINDS OF TERRIBLE

by Peggy Mann

Doubleday & Company, Inc.
Garden City, New York

DESIGNED BY LAURENCE ALEXANDER

Library of Congress Cataloging in Publication Data

Mann, Peggy.
There are two kinds of terrible.

SUMMARY: After his beloved mother dies of cancer, a boy must learn to relate to his father who has withdrawn into his own shell of suffering.
[1. Death–Fiction. 2. Mothers and sons–Fiction. 3. Fathers and sons–Fiction]
I. Cuffari, Richard, 1925– II. Title.
PZ7.M31513Ti [Fic]
Library of Congress Catalog Card Number 76–42372
ISBN 0-385-09588-0 Trade
0-385-08185-5 Prebound

PRINTED IN THE UNITED STATES OF AMERICA

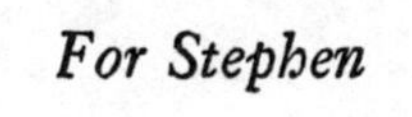

For Stephen

There Are Two Kinds of Terrible

1

It seemed as though the afternoon *knew* that school was out and ten weeks of nothing but summertime lay ahead. The sky was spread with sunshine and when we got to the woods there was this deep sweet smell which comes there after a rain. It makes you want to keep breathing in.

We were on our bikes, Jud and me. Jud lives next door. We're together all the time. Not *because* he lives next door. But because we're two the same. You know what I mean? Like sometimes I'll know what Jud is thinking and I'll answer him—before he even says anything out loud. It's weird.

Anyhow, we were biking along a path in the woods on the first afternoon of the summer vacation and I kept singing a line in my head. "I'm sittin' on top of the wo-orld!" I sang it loud in my head, but not *out* loud. (I mean, even with your best friend you can't act *too* crazy.) I sang that one line because it's all I knew of the song. I heard it on one of those TV commercials for records that they don't sell in the stores. You send your money to some box number. And they try to tempt you up by playing one line from this song and one line from that. But I didn't need to know any more than that one line—because it said everything. I *was* sittin' on top of the world.

You see, aside from school being out and it being this great-looking and great-smelling day, I had this new bike. Well, it wasn't exactly new. Buzzy Carter who lives down the block gave it to me when he got his new ten-speed. This was a three-speed. And it was secondhand when Buzzy first got it. But why I say it was new is, I'd stripped the rusty fenders off and I'd sprayed it with red spray paint, and I'd polished up all the aluminum parts, and I had a new seat put on it. The bike looked new. And it was new to me.

But the brakes weren't new. They were tight to squeeze.

Anyway, here we were whizzing along on this path through the woods, me singing that line to myself and smelling the springtime in the wet leaves and grass and listening to the trickle sound of the stream which flows along near the path, when suddenly I saw it. A fat log on the path. I squeezed on the brakes and tried to make an S-curve. But the brakes didn't answer. I couldn't turn. The bike hit the log hard and I flew over the handlebars.

When I landed, I heard something snap. But I didn't

pay much attention. Not then. I just lay there staring up at the spaces of sky I could see through the leaves.

Jud got off his bike and ran up to me. "You okay?" he said. He sounded more worried than I felt.

"Sure," I said. "Just shook up." I started to sit. My right arm didn't come along with the rest of me, so I kind of lifted it with my left hand. But my arm just fell back.

"It looks broke," Jud said.

"Yeah," I said. I mean I still sounded just casual. But I didn't feel that way. I was scared. The first thing that came into my head like a cold piece of steel shooting through was that my arm would have to be amputated. I don't know why I thought that. I mean, I know broken arms can be set. But this thing of mine looked so gruesome and unattached to the rest of me that it seemed like they would have to just cut it off and be done with it.

"You want me to get your mom?" Jud said.

"Yeah," I said. I lay back in the wet leaves. I was feeling so tired and kind of sick at my stomach. "Yeah, get her. Get her down here quick."

He took off.

With my left hand I was fingering these wet wood chips that they put on the trail to prevent erosion or something. I closed my eyes, thinking maybe I'd go to sleep till my mom got there. Then I opened my eyes to pray up to heaven that she wasn't at the supermarket or someplace. (When I was a real little kid I used to kneel by the bed and all that corny stuff and close my eyes when I prayed. And when I got bigger I stopped praying except for a quickie here and there: Please God, let me do okay on this math test even though I didn't study too good. Little throwaway lines like that. But now I *needed* to pray. And I guess I felt it would be more direct if I opened my eyes and stared right up at the place where God is supposed to be.)

"Let her come quick," I kept saying over and over right out loud.

My pinkie on my right hand started to hurt like crazy. My arm still didn't hurt much, but then I looked at it and that made it hurt because it looked so bad. And suddenly I heard myself screaming, "I want my mommy. I want my mommy." Yeah, just like a dumb little kid of six, there I was lying on my back in the wet leaves staring up at the branches which seemed very high above and screaming out, "I want my mommy."

And then, suddenly, there she was. And Jud too. I didn't even care if Jud heard me screaming out. I was deep-down scared and all I cared about was that my mom should come and take charge of things. And that's what she did.

She knew just what to do. She always seemed to know just what to do if something bad happened. And I don't only mean nurse kind of things. All kind of things.

Anyway, as I later learned, she had been in the kitchen reading the directions for her new crock pot (that's what my dad gave her for her birthday, a crock pot!) when Jud came racing in to tell her what had happened to me. So my mom got some masking tape from the desk, and a pillowcase, and she grabbed up Sunday's newspaper (which my dad always keeps around to read through the whole week). Then she and Jud got in the car and my mom drove like hell to the edge of the woods and she followed Jud, running, down the path—to me.

I can't remember too much of what happened then. As soon as she got there I guess I felt *Now she'll take over*. And I went kind of out. I didn't pass out. But I was just so deep-through tired. My pinkie was still hurting like crazy. But not enough to keep me awake. That's all I wanted—just to fall into a dead sleep.

Of course, my mom couldn't let that happen because she wouldn't be able to carry me, even with Jud helping. She kept saying, "Don't go to sleep, Robbie. Not yet, Pumpkin." (That was a name she used to call me when I was a little kid six years old.) And she kept saying, "It'll be all right, son. Everything will be okay." And while she was talking she was rolling up newspaper and putting masking tape around it. And then she took the pillowcase and ripped it and she and Jud sort of sat me up (I felt like one of those floppy Raggedy Andy dolls) and she turned the rolled-up newspapers into a splint and the torn pillowcase into a sling.

Then, directing Jud on what to do, she and him got me to my feet and somehow we all managed to stagger and stumble down that wet path of leaves and slidy wood chips. I was scared I'd fall again and break the other arm. But we made it to the car.

Mom got me into the back seat. I was half sitting,

half lying. And she put Jud in there to hold me in place like a human seat belt. Jud seemed almost as scared as me. He just did what she told him, like he was a robot who couldn't talk.

"You'll be okay, Pumpkin," my mom said. I opened my eyes and looked at her. I remember the way she smiled. Her face was very white. But her smile was regular.

She closed the door to the back seat gently. And she got behind the wheel. We took off with such a jolt that I screamed out. My arm hurt like it was shot with fire.

"Sorry, Robbie," she said.

Then—Jud told me later—I passed out cold. Which was just as well. Because I guess if I hadn't of passed out, I would have busted out crying like a baby. And that is something you don't want to do—not even in front of your best friend.

2

Operation.

That was the word that sliced through all the haze and daze and aching of my arm.

"What do I need an *operation* for?" I almost shouted the words at Dr. Gregory. I mean, I know plenty of kids —well, three anyway—who've broken an arm or a leg and all *they* got was a cast. So why did *I* need an *operation?*

Dr. Gregory told me why. In fact, he showed me the X rays he had just taken. They were still wet, so he didn't touch them. But he held them in front of this strong light and he pointed out the thin white line in the bone. "You did a good job, Robbie," he said. "That's no simple fracture. It's a rugged break. We'll have to set it with metal plates screwed into the bone. That's why we'll have to operate. You'll be in the hospital about eight days."

"Great," I said in a sour voice. I mean here Jud and me were planning to start our tennis lessons the next day. And where would I be? In the hospital with metal plates in my arm. My right arm. My tennis arm.

"I know," Dr. Gregory said, trying to sound sympathetic. "The first day of summer vacation is not the best time in the world for breaking your arm. But—I guess all you can do is grin and bear it. And be glad it wasn't any worse."

"Yeah," I said, still sourer, "sure!"

My mom called for a cab to take Jud home. Then she drove me from the Medical Building where Dr. Gregory worked, to the hospital. Dr. Gregory said he'd come along as soon as they phoned him that I was all checked in and ready for the operation.

He'd given me a painkiller shot in his office, so I was kind of groggy. When I got to bed in the hospital room all I wanted was to sleep. My mom was somewhere filling out forms about the insurance and stuff. She'd told me she would be in to stay with me as soon as she was done. And I sure wished she'd hurry up, because there was this rotten kid in the next bed. I couldn't see how old he was because he was under the covers. And I didn't want to ask how old he was, because I didn't want to talk to him. All I wanted was that he should shut up. But he kept on talking even though I didn't answer. Now that I look back on it, I guess he was having some kind of fun, passing the time by scaring me to death. But right then—all groggy and slowed down in my mind, I believed everything he was saying.

"The doctors here are mean," he said. "Real deep down mean. And the nurses are even worse. You're lucky if you get out of this place alive."

He told me that he'd been rock climbing with his father and he fell off a cliff and had to have twenty stitches sewn in his head. Maybe that affected his brains or something. I mean why else would you want to scare a person who was waiting to have an operation?

Then he started asking me about my collar bone. I didn't even know where my collar bone *was*, so I couldn't say whether it was broke or not when he asked me. So then the kid says, "You just better hope it's not broke, because I know a guy who got real creamed from riding his bike. He broke his collar bone and he got paralyzed from the neck down."

"Is that right?" I said, trying to sound just cool like we were talking about the weather.

And then these two men in white kind of robes came in and lifted me out of the bed and onto this narrow table on wheels.

"Where you taking me?" I said. My voice didn't sound like *my* voice. No one there knew what my voice sounded like, so maybe they didn't hear how different it was from being scared. But I didn't even recognize my own voice.

"To the operating room," one of the men said. Then

he looked at a clipboard he was carrying. "You're Robert Farley, aren't you?"

"They got to check that they got the right body," this reject in the next bed says. "They've been known to cut off the wrong leg of the wrong person around here."

"All right, Snyder," the man with the clipboard said. "Enough!"

It sounded like they were wise to this squirt. And fed up with him.

"I'm Robert Farley," I said to the two men. "But my mom said she'd be here before they took me away to operate on."

"Well, I'm sorry, son," Clipboard said. "We work on a tight schedule around here. When we're sent to get someone, we can't wait around."

He said it in a nice way, and I nodded like I understood. But, when a kid is going in to have his arm cut open you'd think they could just stall around for a little bit till his mom can get there and kiss him good-by at least.

And then, just as they started wheeling me out the door—she came!

"Oh, Mom," I said. That's all I said. But I was saying a lot more than just those two words.

"It'll be okay, Robbie." She held my hand. "Don't worry, Pumpkin. I'll be right here every minute. I'll be waiting in the room when you get back. Daddy'll be here too. I phoned him in the office and he's taking the next train."

"Dad's coming?" I felt a little surprised. I don't know why. I mean, why shouldn't he come when his only kid has to have an operation with metal plates screwed into his bones? Along with feeling surprised, I felt pleased.

"We've got to take him now, Mrs. Farley," Clipboard said.

"Can I walk along with him to the operating room?" my mom asked.

But Clipboard shook his head. "Regulations," he said.

So my mom kissed me on the forehead. "I love you," she whispered, so that only I could hear. I mean, I know she loved me. But she didn't say it often.

I was glad she said it then.

They must have given me something to knock me out because all I remember is staring at the ceiling lights as they were wheeling me through some hallway. And I woke up in the recovery room. Some old guy was shouting out about how the bandages hurt his back. And I had this little rubber hose thing sticking into my arm and attached to a bottle hanging over the bed. And there was this heavy cast on my arm. It reached from the middle of my shoulder to the middle of my hand. I tried to move my fingers a little. It hurt like hell.

This old guy kept screaming around. (I guess it's not only kids that scream. Or maybe even old guys get turned back to kids inside when they're hurting a lot. Anyway, I wished he'd shut up. I felt real groggy and my arm was hurting and I wanted to go back to sleep.)

A nurse came and asked how I was feeling and I asked her where was my mom.

"I guess she'll be waiting in your room," the nurse said.

"What room?" I said. "Where am I now?"

"The recovery room." She had some chart on a clipboard too. She looked at it and started away.

"I want to get out of here," I said, loud, to stop her leaving. "I want to go back to my room right now."

She came back to the bed. She told me that I could go to my room after all the glucose had drained out of that hanging bottle, and into me. She explained it so I knew what was what. But the sound of her voice wasn't too nice. It was like she was saying: Look, you dumb kid, I got a lot more important customers than you to pay attention to. So just lie there and be quiet.

Then she went over to the old guy who was still carrying on about how his back hurt and the dressings were on wrong and he wanted to see his doctor.

She talked to him in the same kind of grouchy voice that she talked to me. I mean, her words were nice enough. If someone called her up in front of the chief nurse and repeated the words, no one could blame her for a thing. But the way she said the words made you feel like some kind of jerk because you were hurting and wanted someone to do something about it.

After she left, the old guy looked over at me and he said, "Sister of Mercy!"

"Yeah!" I said.

Then he started yelling out again about his back and the bandages. But this time I didn't hate him. I felt we were together in our pain against them. I guess it was being angry at him that had kept me awake, not the sound of his screaming. Anyway, when I wasn't angry any more I fell right asleep.

When I woke up my wrist watch said six o'clock. I thought it was six in the night. Then a nurse came in—this one was pretty—and she stuck a thermometer in my mouth. "Good morning!" she said in a cheery voice. "Sleep well?" That was what gave me kind of a clue that it was six in the morning.

The next bed was empty. I was glad that rotten kid had gone. But where was my mom?

I said to the nurse, "My mother said she'd be here when I woke up."

The nurse—whose name turned out to be Miss Solomon—gave me a nice smile. "Your mother *was* here, honey. And your dad too. They stayed last night till visiting hours were over. Stayed right here by your bed, even though you were out like a light. The doctor told them you probably wouldn't wake up till morning. Even so they stayed. Just in case."

"Oh," I said. I felt a lot better. Even my dad had stayed!

Then this Miss Solomon took my pulse and plumped my pillows and asked me if I wanted some breakfast.

There was a TV set hanging from heavy wires high

over the foot of my bed. I asked her how to work the thing. There was this little box by my bed and she showed me how to press the buttons to turn the TV on and off and switch the channels. It was neat. The only trouble, 6 A.M. must be the prime time for boring programs. One channel had some guy lecturing about rocks and stuff. Another channel had some weirdo with a pointer standing by a blackboard and he was carrying on about the pancreas. I mean who wants to learn about the pancreas at 6 A.M.?

Then, sharp at nine, when visiting hours open, guess who came!

My dad.

It's like when you lift up a glass to take a drink and you're expecting it to be milk but it turns out to be tomato juice or Coke or something. Whatever it is, even if you like it, it tastes funny at first—because you're all set to taste milk. You know what I mean?

Anyway, that's how it was. I was all set inside to see Mom. And Dad walked in.

"Oh!" I said. And my surprise sounded right out loud in my voice. "Hi."

Maybe you wonder why I should be surprised to see my own dad at nine o'clock the morning after an operation.

I'll tell you why.

3

I mean I love my dad. He's my father, after all. And he's always been perfectly nice to me. But like he's in his world and I'm in mine and it's not only that those two worlds are far apart. But his world *keeps* him apart.

He's usually gone by the time I get up in the morning because he has to make an early train. Our place is a fifty-minute train ride from the city where Dad works as a C.P.A. Don't ask me what a C.P.A. *does* exactly. I've asked my dad and all he ever says is, "Oh, taxes and things." Around income tax time each year he gets so busy that he doesn't even come home at all. He sleeps over at a hotel in the city.

When it's not income tax time, he gets home around seven-thirty at night. Then he has a drink and he's not ready for dinner till eight o'clock.

Well, I happen to have this huge appetite. Even if I

have a big snack when I get home from school, I still can't hold out till eight o'clock. And on the weekends, if I did eat dinner with them, my dad talked about his kind of things, not my kind of things. I mean, he's very into politics and world affairs and all that stuff. He'd say things to me like: "How's school?" and "How's your friend, Jud?" And I'd make some one word answer like, "Okay," or "Great." It didn't seemed to matter to him what I answered. Asking me some question about my world was just a ritual he went through, like washing his hands before he sat down to eat. So we'd have our two little sentences, and then he'd close himself back into his world again. And my mom went with him.

I didn't ever blame her for that. I mean, she was with me plenty. She'd have breakfast with me in the morning. And since I live close to school I'd come home for lunch. And she was there then. And when I got home from school, we'd have a snack together. She was more than just *there*. She *wanted* to know what was happening in my world.

But I started telling about my dad. How'd my mom get here in the act?

Jud says my dad is kind of a cold fish. Which about sums it up. I don't get insulted that he says this about my dad. Because he says the same exact thing about his dad. And when he doesn't say it about his dad, I say it. That's one of the things which brings Jud and me close. We both have this same kind of cold-fish dad.

It's like each of them forgot the time when they

were boys. In fact, it's even hard to believe they ever *were* boys. If I try to think of my dad as a boy, all I can do is imagine him looking just like he does now, only with more hair, and about a quarter the size.

To tell you the truth, I don't know why my dad ever had me. I'm sure I was one hundred per cent my mom's idea. I can even imagine them talking about it. My mom: "Reggie"—Yeah, that's his name! What a name to load on someone. Reginald. Maybe that's half his problem. —"Reggie, I get lonesome at home all alone. Either I want to go back to work or I want to have a child to occupy my time."

And my dad (who, by the way, is Mr. Anti-Women's Lib in person): "Well, I don't want you going back to work, *that's* for sure! So I might as well settle for the second choice. Okay, we'll have a kid."

I'm sure that's the way I happened.

Anyway, like I was saying, on school nights, since I got too hungry to wait till eight o'clock, my mom always let me have my dinner in my room so I could watch TV. (I have my own set. When they got a color set in their bedroom, they let me have the old black and white.)

When my dad got home he'd call up to me, "Hi, Robbie." And I'd call back down to him, "Hi, Dad." And that was about it. Sometimes, he'd make the big effort and call another sentence up to me. "How was school?" Or, "Have a good day?" And that *was* it. (Or, at least it was

—until everything suddenly changed at the end of the year.)

On weekends, well, some dads who commute make up for lost time you might say. They'll get out and play ball with their son. I've even seen a father get down on the floor and play Monopoly with his kids. But for my dad weekends were for doing chores and for seeing friends. His friends. (It always kind of surprises me, but he does have quite a lot of friends. And they seem to like him. Well, he knows all this stuff about politics and the stock market. I guess this makes him interesting to some people. Also, according to my mom, he has this wonderful dry wit. I must say I never see much sign of it. I guess it only comes out with his friends. One of whom is Jud's father, as you might imagine.)

So, like on Saturday morning my dad would drive Mom to the supermarket. He likes to shop around for the things that *he* likes to eat. (Well, since he's paying for the stuff, who can blame him after all, if he picks out what he wants. I mean, he ***really*** enjoys that. "Browsing in the aisles," he calls it.) What I like is to push the cart, and go scooting around on it. But on Saturday mornings the aisles are too crowded to do any scooting. And my father's always telling me I'll tip over the cart and I should stop. (During the weekday afternoons if I went to the supermarket with Mom I'd always scoot on the cart. I'm good at it. I put one foot on the bottom rung, and push off with my other foot and lean my weight on the front with my arms. And whiz down the aisles. I never once did tip the cart over. Though a couple of times I banged into a shopper by accident. At those times my mom pretended I wasn't with her!)

On Saturday afternoons I mostly spent the time with my own friends. And on Saturday nights my dad and mom would either go out to their friends, or they'd have people in. Then I got to be introduced and to serve peanuts with the drinks. And that's about it. As soon as I could I always headed for my room. (Some of my best TV shows are on Saturday nights.)

On Sunday afternoons Dad usually just plunked himself in his leather armchair and read through the different sections of the Sunday paper. You'd think Mom would have been bored out of her mind on Sunday afternoons. But maybe when they were alone together some of my dad's dry wit showed. Or something.

Well, the whole point I'm trying to make in telling all this is that it wasn't exactly my dad I was looking to see when I came to after that operation. And I guess I didn't hide my feelings any too well—because when he walked into my hospital room and said in a real jolly voice, "Well, how's my boy this morning?" all I could think to answer was: "Where's Mom?"

Maybe my dad was kind of insulted that I didn't even tell him I was glad to see him. He let me know right off that he was taking a later train this morning so that he could stop in at the hospital first.

"Thanks, Dad," I said. "I appreciate that."

He kind of smiled at me, and pulled up a chair.

"Well, how was it?" he said.

"How was what?"

"The operation."

"Oh," I said. "Well, I kind of feel like I wasn't there."

"I know," he said. "That's how I felt when I had my operation."

"When did you have an operation, Dad?" I said. (I was interested. I know all these corny jokes about people talking about their operations. But no one had ever told me that my dad had an operation. Maybe it would give us something to really be together about.)

"I was operated on long before you were born," my dad said.

"Did you have a broken arm like me?" (I didn't mean to sound so eager. But I kind of felt that way.)

"It was a hernia operation," he said.

(What the hell was a hernia? Something like a pancreas, I guess. I thought of that weirdo with the pointer at the blackboard at 6 A.M. Even my dad's *operation* was boring! I changed the subject.)

"When's Mom coming?"

"She'll be along," he said. "She'll be with you all day if you want her. But I can only stay a little while, so she thought we'd like to have some time alone together."

"Sure, Dad," I said.

I tried to think of something else to talk about. I guess Dad was trying to think too. Anyway, there was this little flat piece of silence when we just looked at each other. Then Dad glanced at his watch. "I don't have to go quite yet," he said.

"That's good," I said. And I suddenly thought of something to talk about. I told him about this creep who had been in the other bed. And I said how I was glad they'd moved him out. Or maybe he'd gotten better. Or maybe they'd kicked him out because nobody could stand him any more.

"Well, let's hope you'll get someone a little more sociable for a roommate," my dad said. He laughed a little.

I laughed a little too.

"I'm sure your own friends will be stopping in to see you," my dad said. "The eight days in the hospital will pass before you even know it."

"I sure hope so!" I said.

Well, the eight days did not pass before I even knew it. They were the slowest-dragging days I could remember. In the pediatric ward they allow kids to visit you—if you've got broken bones or something else not catching. And Jud and some of my other friends did come in to see me. But they were kind of stiff and formal being in a hospital room. The little kid who became my new roommate was only four years old. He slept a lot. And when he wasn't sleeping, he was crying. Whichever way, it put kind of a damper on me and my friends. We either had to talk soft so as not to wake him up, or talk extra loud so we could hear each other over the crying kid. Anyway, by the end of the eight days, none of my friends showed up any more. Except Jud.

My mom was there a lot. But even my mom and me seemed to run out of things to talk about. She brought me presents. Like a game with invisible ink and you rub some powder stuff on what you wrote and it appears. That was my favorite. I made up stories for myself like being a counterspy and stuff.

I got a big package one day from my father's sister, my Aunt Emily, who lives in Muncie, Indiana. I was real excited opening it. And underneath the brown outside wrapping there was this fancy paper wrapping with rabbits hopping all over the green-field background and saying, "Get Well quick, quick, quick," in little white balloons. I even liked the corny wrapping paper. And I liked it that my Aunt Emily had sent it Fourth Class Special Delivery. (Maybe what I liked best about *that* was Miss Solomon coming into my room carrying this package and saying, "Well, guess who has a Special Delivery present!" I mean, I really kind of liked this Miss Solomon and I thought about her a lot.)

The present itself, however, was a big letdown.

It was one of these educational board games. With all these little pieces, and cards, and dice and stuff. *Some* board games are good. I mean, I really dig Monopoly. But most board games, in my opinion, they should call bored games. This was about the Bible.

I mean, that's just what I needed to pass the time. Spinning dice and picking up little cards to teach me about Joshua and Moses. This board game was about the Old Testament, and there was a note at the end of the directions (which I even read—so you can see how desperate I was for something to do!) and the note said that you also could send for a New Testament Bible Game for $7.95, plus tax and mailing charges. (They even included a little chart so you could figure how much the tax and mailing charges were in your state.)

Miss Solomon said she would come and play the Bible game with me one evening after she got off work. And she kept her word. We tried for twenty minutes to figure out the directions. But it was too complicated, so we gave up and she played me a game of Go Fish instead. All *that* takes is a deck of cards.

When I grow up, one of the things I'm going to do on the side is be a board-game tycoon. Maybe I can think of a few good games that'll last through the ages, like Monopoly. (My dad told me even *he* used to play it as a kid!) But whether my games are good or not, I figure I can't help but make a pile of money. I mean, how much can it cost to manufacture a board made out of some crummy pressed cardboard or something, and a few little dice and some cards or a spinner? You stick it all in a box with little partitions. And you wrap the whole thing with cellophane so someone who wants to buy it can't even have a look inside to see what a bunch of nothing he's getting. And then you sell the thing for $7.95. I mean, those board-game makers must really be sitting there splitting their sides laughing at people's dumbness—while *they're* raking in the dough.

Anyway, I wrote my Aunt Emily a nice, polite letter saying how much I was learning about the Bible and that I hoped she'd be coming to visit us sometime soon so that we could play it together. (When I wrote that letter I didn't expect that my wish would come true. In the most terrible way of all.)

5

I guess you can imagine what that summer was like.

Terrible.

First of all, I had the cast on for over six weeks and it was real hot that July and August and the cast began bugging me like crazy. All the sweat would run down inside and it would itch me and it was all grubby and grimy like. I had this walkie-talkie that I'd gotten as a present the Christmas before and I took the aerial off it so I could reach down under the cast and scratch. It didn't help the itchiness too much. All it did was make the cut from the operation sting. But anyway I kept scratching with that aerial. Sometimes my whole arm from my shoulder to my hand was like one big ITCH!

What did I do that summer? I hung around. I watched. I watched Jud take his tennis lessons. I watched other guys play baseball. I sat on the edge of the Community House swimming pool and dangled my feet in the water and watched everyone swimming and diving and splashing around.

I mean there are some kids who are really into reading books and all that. For them it might not be too bad to break an arm in the summertime. But me, I've always been more into sports. That's why I look forward to the summertime so much. Summertime is sports time. No one's expecting you to come in from baseball practice or to stop shooting baskets and do your homework. You're *supposed* to be out of the house in the summertime. Riding your bike. Swimming. Tennis. All those things. The pro at the Community Center had said I was a tennis natural. (A lot better than Jud, if you want to know.) That's why he wanted to start me in on lessons early. I'm tall for my age. And I have a strong right arm. At least, I did have.

That laid me back a lot—Jud taking the tennis lessons; me sitting there. Watching.

There was something else I couldn't do that I was counting on that summer. Play my drum.

My birthday is in April and my mom had given me a snare drum. That's the one with little wire snares on the bottom. They lift up onto the bottom skin and they vibrate on it when you hit the top skin.

Why do I say that my mom had given me the drum for my birthday; not my mom and dad? Let me tell you, I say it for a plenty good reason. My dad didn't want me to have a drum (to put it mildly). He hates loud noise.

My mom tried to make me understand about it. Some people are sensitive to one thing, she said. Like they sneeze from chicken feathers in pillows. And some people upchuck when they eat hazel nuts. And some people are very–sensitive (that's the polite word she used) about noise.

When she got me the snare drum, the agreement was that I wouldn't play it while Dad was home. That meant no playing after seven-thirty on week nights, and no playing during Sunday newspaper-reading time. What it also meant was that plenty of times I'd get this real charged-up feeling of wanting to practice on the drum and I'd have to try to shove the feeling away. Because of Dad. Only often the feeling didn't *go* away. It just turned into anger.

Anyhow, you can see why I'd been looking forward to the summer so far as drum playing was concerned. I'd have the whole day to beat my heart out any time I wanted. (Mom didn't mind my practicing. She said it sounded exciting. I'd have my record player on and I'd drum along in time to the music, the two sticks going like crazy. Sometimes I'd just have to laugh out loud, it sounded so good, and it made me feel so good.)

When the summertime came I planned to practice a couple of hours every day. ("Practice" may sound boring. Like when I was taking piano lessons with that smelly-breath Miss Stimpson. But when you're talking about the drums, practice is wild, man. It's fun!)

Anyway, you can imagine how much drumming I

got done during those eight weeks with a cast on my right arm from my shoulder to the middle of my hand!

Well, I guess you're not too fascinated hearing the gloomy details of all the things I couldn't do that hang-around, arm-itching summer. When I say that I was really looking forward to school—I mean, I was actually counting the days till school would *begin*—then I guess you'll know how terrible that summer was!

A couple of weeks before school started, Dr. Gregory took off the cast. Somehow, I thought the scar would be some nice neat little pink line on my arm. Well, let me tell you—it was gruesome! This thick, ugly, scabby-looking thing.

Since it was still steamy-hot in September and I wasn't about to wear long-sleeved shirts, I had the added pleasure of perfect strangers coming up to me in the supermarket, in school, and places, and saying, "What *happened* to you?" Maybe they think a kid doesn't get embarrassed and fed up and mad with people staring at his scar, and asking dumb questions. Let me tell you, a kid is just like anyone else about such matters. I mean, who, for example, would sail up to my piano teacher (*ex*-piano teacher!) Miss Stimpson and say: "My goodness, how did you get that terrible scar?" It would be bad manners, wouldn't it? But people seem to think a kid doesn't have those kind of feelings.

Anyway, as the school year went on, things began to get better. First off, I had a great teacher. Mr. Jenson.

He's high on muscles. He's got this gym right in his apartment. And he's really strong. He can take two kids and lift them up by their belts at the same time, like they're dumbbells or something. (The iron kind of dumbbells.) He jogs four miles a day around the reservoir before school which means he gets up at five o'clock every weekday morning. Things like that.

Well, Mr. Jenson, being kind of a sports nut himself, understood how I felt not being able to go out for football, or any kind of contact sports. I mean, I still had these plates and screws in the bone of my right arm, so I had to be careful. You know what I had to sign up for the first semester in sports: *Ping Pong!* And even that kind of made my arm ache.

Anyway, Mr. Jenson took a special interest in getting me interested in other things aside from sports. Like he got me to sign up for chorus. I found out I have a pretty good singing voice. And that gave me the idea to start my own band when I get old enough. I can be the vocalist and the drummer. And because it'll be my band, it'll have my name. The band will be called: The Robs. I don't exactly know why, but I really dig that name.

Not being able to go out for football practice after school meant that I had more time for two things. One was to practice on my snare drum (with cut-off time at seven-thirty, when Dad got home). The other was—just rapping with my mom. I can't even tell you what we talked about so much. My band. School. Even jerky-sounding things like what I want to be when I grow up.

Mostly we didn't talk deep. We talked light. We laughed a lot. I mean, most guys I know, their mom is just a mother. Like my dad is a father. He wins the bread and goes off in the train to his office and comes home and calls up to me, "Hi, Robbie." He's there, that's all. I have no complaints. But I got no real reasons to turn handsprings either.

I guess to my mom though he was a lot different, because he really loved her. I mean, even I can tell that. Sometimes he'd just look at her, and give her a warm kind of smile. Just for nothing.

That's why I felt surprised the first time I heard them arguing.

I mean, they never had fights. Mostly, I guess it's because my mom gave into him. Or, got around him.

So you can see when I heard them arguing loud enough so their voices reached up to the second floor, through the closed door of my room, and past the sound of my TV program, naturally I felt kind of uneasy. Some kids, their parents are at each other all the time, so when it happens it's one big nothing: there they go again. But when *my* parents did it—it was scary.

The first time it happened, I just turned my TV up louder. It didn't want to hear. I guess I figured if I didn't hear, it didn't happen.

But it did happen. The next night, the same thing. This time, instead of tuning out by turning up the TV sound, I opened the door of my room and hollered down, "Hey, what are you two arguing about?"

There was like this dead silence.

Then my mom called up to me, "We're not arguing, honey."

That was even more scary than their hot voices going at each other. I mean my mom was always straight with me; she always told me the truth. So how come she was telling me they weren't arguing when they sure as hell were?

Then my dad put in his two bits. "We're just having a–difference of opinion, son."

Maybe it was politics or something. I shrugged one shoulder and closed my door. I wanted to play my drum to get some of the worry out of me. But it was after hours for drum playing. So I went back to my TV. It was a comedy program and I laughed on cue when the canned laughing came. But don't ask me what I was laughing about. I kept thinking that maybe my mom and dad were going to split up or something. Plenty of kids in my class have parents who are divorced. But I sure didn't want it to happen to me.

The arguing kept up each night.

Turned out it wasn't anything about divorce. I didn't find out what the arguing was all about until much later. When it was too late.

One day when I came home from school for lunch my mom said, "Take your key when you leave, Pumpkin. I may not be home when school's out."

It's funny but what struck me then was that she called me Pumpkin. She hadn't called me that little-boy name since the day I broke my arm.

"Where you going?" I asked her.

"I have to have my checkup."

"What kind of checkup?" I asked her. "Your driving test?"

"My yearly medical checkup," she said.

"Oh," I said.

"Everyone has a yearly medical checkup," she said in an easy voice. But somehow her just saying that made me *un*easy.

She looked at her watch and right in the middle of

me eating my grilled cheese sandwich she said, "Matter of fact, I'm running late. I'd better get a move on." She stood up.

"What time will you be home?" I asked her.

"Not sure," she said. "You know the way they keep you waiting around for these tests and all."

"Sure," I said. "I know." I was trying to sound real with it. After all, I'd been kept waiting around plenty in the hospital with my arm.

At the front door she called back to me, "There's just a slight chance that I might have to stay over for some tests. But if I do, I'll phone you. Bye-bye, Pumpkin."

"Bye," I said, and I swallowed down hard on my grilled cheese. Somehow I didn't *like* her calling me Pumpkin. Not now when my arm was out of its cast and I was back in a pretty much regular life again.

And she didn't even come in to kiss me good-by like she usually did when she took off. It was like she couldn't wait to be on her way.

Usually I love grilled cheese. But now I felt that if I ate it, the sandwich would just sit there in my stomach like it was made out of lead. I heard the front door slam. And I pushed the sandwich away.

Then the telephone rang.

I jumped up.

Why? What's so scary about a phone ringing?

I snatched up the receiver. "Hello," I said.

"Hello," a lady's voice said. "Has Mrs. Farley left for the hospital yet?"

"Hospital?" I said. "I don't know anything about any hospital." (I mean *I* go for my medical checkups to Dr. Greenberg at the Medical Building on Oakdale Avenue. They got everything there. An eye doctor. An ear, nose, and throat doctor. A pediatrician (Dr. Greenberg). A bone doctor (Gregory). I mean they got the whole works there. Plus X-ray machines and everything. So why would she need to go to the *hospital* for a yearly checkup?

Then this lady—I guess she was a nurse—says a real dumb thing. "Ooops," she goes, "I wasn't supposed to say that, was I?"

"Wasn't supposed to say *what?*" I said.

"Are you the son?" she says.

"Yeah," I said.

"Oh," she says. "Well—thank you, dear." And she hangs up.

I mean I felt real chills running through me.

Hospital . . . Ooops . . . I wasn't supposed to say that, was I? Are you the son?

The whole thing was kind of weird.

Since I didn't want any more lunch and since the house seemed very empty and since I was feeling this shaky way inside I ran upstairs, shut the door of my room, and started hitting my drum.

I mean, why didn't she tell me she was going to the *hospital* for tests? Maybe she just forgot.

Somehow I knew that she wouldn't be home that night. And I was right.

When Dad came home I didn't know what to do.

I mean, I'd eaten ahead, like usual. (*What* I ate wasn't like usual. I had two cans of Coke. Mom doesn't let me have Coke for dinner. She says the caffeine will keep me awake. And I had a salami sandwich. And that was it. Mom is kind of a nutrition nut. Meat. *Fresh* vegetables. Some of them she even grows herself in the garden. Anyway, she believes in "a good well-balanced dinner." For lunch she lets me have pretty much what I want. That's how come we even have salami and Coke in the fridge.)

Anyway, Dad called up like usual when he came in, "Hi, Robbie."

And I called back, "Hi, Dad."

Then he opened up some. "How's the boy?" he called.

"Fine," I called back down.

And that was it. He went on into the kitchen. I heard him potzing around down there. He's not much of a cook. (Although in the summer he does make good steaks on the backyard barbecue.) Also, he isn't much of a mechanic. Whenever he tries the electric can opener, he ends up swearing at it.

I decided I'd go down and ask about Mom and I found him swearing at the can opener. He was trying to open a can of mushroom soup.

"How come Mom didn't come home tonight?" I asked, real easy like. Then I said, "Here. Let me." And I took the can of soup from him and pressed down in a certain crooked way on the can opener—which *is* kind of temperamental. But Mom had showed me where to press and how hard.

"Your mother has to have a few tests," he said. "Ones they do early in the morning. Before breakfast. So they thought it would be better if she stayed the night."

"What *kind* of tests?" I asked.

Dad shrugged. "A battery of tests, that's all they told me." Then he smiled a little. "They don't tell you much, these doctors, do they?"

"They sure don't." I said.

It may sound crazy, but this was the closest kind of talk between us that I could remember.

"Do you like your mushroom soup made with milk or water?" I asked him.

"Milk, please," my dad said.

I made him his whole dinner while he sat at the kitchen table reading the paper. Soup. Ravioli. Sliced tomatoes. Tea. And yogurt for dessert. He seemed to sort of appreciate my getting his dinner, and just—being there. I mean I had the feeling that though he was looking at the paper, he wasn't all that taken up with what he was reading. You know?

After he ate we phoned Mom. Talking to her made all the kind of worry inside me just sail right out like a blown up balloon. She was her exact same cheery self. I know if she'd have been worried about anything, it would have shown in her voice.

Even though I didn't feel worried I asked, "What kind of tests do you have to stay overnight for?"

"Just routine tests," she told me.

"But what *kind* of tests, Mom?"

"Women kind," she said. "You wouldn't know what they were if I told you."

"Oh," I said. "Well . . . okay, then."

She asked about my homework and I told her that I didn't have any. (Mr. Jenson's not big on homework.) And she asked about Jud and about this new kid in my class named Simon who everyone was being mean to just because he was new. We had the same kind of talk we'd have had if she'd of been home.

When I hung up I wondered whether most mothers have those kind of women-tests. I thought about asking my dad this. But I decided not to.

I went to bed my regular time. And I called down, like usual, "I'm going to bed now. G'night."

My dad called back, like usual, "G'night, Rob."

I kind of wondered whether he'd come upstairs and tuck me in like my mom always did. I figured he wouldn't. And I figured right.

The next day everything was back to regular. My mom was there when I got home from school. I gave her a big hug and told her I'd missed her. Then I got out some Coke and potato chips and sat at the kitchen table while Mom shelled peas—yeah, peas from our garden—and I told her about school and stuff. And it seemed crazy that I should have been so worried the night before. Here she was. Just like always. Everything just exactly like it had always been.

Except it wasn't.

Two days later when I got home from school Mom was waiting for me. And she had a small suitcase by the front door, all packed.

She was still her cheery self. But what she said wasn't so exactly cheery.

"Now it's my turn, Pumpkin," she said.

"Turn for what?"

"An operation. Just a very minor one," she added quickly.

"Oh," I said.

"It's nothing at all to worry about," my mom said. "But I figured I might as well get it over and done with as soon as possible."

"What's—wrong with you?" I said. My voice sounded kind of scratchy. I mean my mom was hardly ever sick. And even if she *was* sick, she wouldn't admit it. She always said staying in bed just made her feel worse. When it was a matter of me, of course, it was something else again! First the thermometer popped in the mouth. Then the telephone call to Dr. Greenberg. But for herself, she hated doctors. So what was her big rush now to get herself to the hospital? Suitcase all packed and everything!

"What's wrong with me?" my mom said. "Just one of those women's things."

"Oh," I said.

She didn't seem worried. So why should I be?

She told me since they had a bed available, they wanted her there right away. She had only waited for me to get home.

"Does Dad know?" I said.

"The doctor phoned him at the office. Dad will probably come straight from the station to the hospital to-night. So if you want to invite Jud over for supper—"

"I want to come to the hospital too," I said.

"You can't, lovey. No visitors under sixteen years old."

I guess I scowled or something.

"I'll be home before you know it," my mom said.

"*When?*"

She shrugged. "Probably I'll be in for a shorter time than you were."

"You call that short?" I burst out. "Eight days! It was like forever."

"When you're in it might seem slow," my mom said. "But for those going on with their regular lives—it goes quickly. You'll see, Pumpkin."

Why did she keep calling me that six-year-old name all of a sudden?

"Maybe," my mom said, "you'd like to have some of your friends for a sleep-over Saturday night."

"Sure! Okay!" I said. "But—what's Dad going to say about that?" (With his thing against noise he's usually not too thrilled up about my having guys sleep over. Four or five boys in one room has just got to mean noise.)

"Don't worry," my mom said. "I'll talk to him. He'll be at the hospital anyway till visiting hours are over. He'll be glad you're living it up a little."

"Maybe," I said.

She laughed. "I'll be glad anyway." Then she looked at her watch. "I better be getting down there instead of rapping here with you." She picked up her suitcase.

I took it from her, and we walked together to the car.

She was wearing a yellow sweater—the one I got her for her birthday, and a plaid skirt. And she had on stockings and her good black shoes. I wondered why she'd wear party shoes to go to an operation.

Before I hardly knew what was happening, she had kissed me good-by, and she was in the car and backing out of the driveway.

"GOOD-BY, MOM," I called, real loud.

She waved at me with one hand out the open window.

I ran down the driveway after her.

And then I just stood there as my mom drove away down the dirt road, and disappeared around the bend.

8

I made this secret chart and I kept it under my pillow. Eight days till she'd be back. Eight empty squares. When I went to bed each night I blacked in another square.

Each day I had a long talk with her when I came home for lunch. The wall telephone in the kitchen has a fifteen-foot extension, so I could stretch it all the way to the kitchen table and I'd be talking to Mom while I ate my salami and rye and Coke (my favorite lunch). It wasn't too different from usual. In fact, if I closed my eyes while I ate I could even imagine her right in the kitchen with me. I guess anyone looking in the kitchen window those times would have thought I was some kind of nut. Me sitting there eating a sandwich with my eyes tight closed. But when you know you're alone you can do some pretty crazy-looking things, and they seem—okay, you know?

When I got home from school, it was the same thing. I'd call her up. I couldn't always get her then. If she was sleeping, she'd unplug her phone. Or sometimes the nurse would answer and say, "Mrs. Farley is not in the room at present." Then I'd keep calling till Mom answered again. When I asked where she'd been, she'd just say—in the lounge or somewhere like that. She told me she got fed up staying in her room. And I bought that. I sure got fed up staying in the room during *my* eight days.

Dad went to the hospital straight from the train station every night. He had his dinner there in the cafeteria, and then he'd stay with Mom till closing time.

It was kind of lonesome for me with no one in the house. But, on the other hand, it wasn't too exactly different from the way things had been before Mom went for her operation. I mean, I ate by the TV in my room the way I used to. And when Dad got home, he'd call up, "Hi, Robbie." And I'd call down, "Hi, Dad," the way I used to.

But then, since I wanted to hear about Mom, I'd come down and ask him how she was. He'd say she was coming along okay and then he'd ask me about school. Not like he wanted too much to know. More like he was asking me questions Mom had told him to ask me. Her kind of questions. About the new boy, Simon, and were the kids being any nicer to him. About Buzzy Carter and did he get to be captain of the basketball team. About how I did on my English test. Things like that.

I gave him the answers, but not long answers like I

gave Mom. Little answers, because I knew he didn't really want to know.

On Saturday night, like Mom had suggested, I had four guys in for a sleep-over.

It was kind of weird. Did you ever do all the things you do when you have a good time? Other people have a good time doing those exact same things. Only somehow, *you* don't. That's how it was.

I mean the food was great. (Much better than if Mom had been there.) Jud and I went shopping for it on Saturday afternoon. We had to take a bus to the supermarket since there was no one to drive us. My dad left for the hospital real early that morning.

We bought a whole pile of junk food. For meat we had hot dogs. (My mom once read this article about how inspectors found rat hairs and cockroach eggs in a hot-dog factory so she never bought hot dogs after that. Because of the article I picked out kosher hot dogs. Kosher means this Jewish inspector guy comes along and kind of blesses the hot dogs. I figured if there was any rats running around the Jewish hot-dog factory, this kosher guy would see them and call in the exterminator. And they taste just as good as the not-Jewish kind, so why not buy them?)

Also, we bought a couple of cans of yellow cheese stuff that oozes out like yellow worms when you press this plastic lever at the top of the can. And of course we bought a lot of Cokes and potato chips.

Jud and I were together all day. At seven o'clock the others came. Buzzy and Fred and this kid from a grade above us named Red Sykes. He's our same age but he's too smart for our grade so they skipped him. Only his brain is bigger than his size if you know what I mean. He's littler than most of the boys in our class. Also, he's kind of backward social-wise. So he has no friends in his grade, which is why he hangs out with us. When you grow up it must be a help to be a brain. But for a kid it can be a real pain.

Anyhow, we had this real good meal (on paper plates so we wouldn't have any dishes to wash).

Then we just watched TV and messed around. The others seemed to be having a ball. But somehow I felt kind of—thin inside. You know? Also, I felt like I wasn't all there. Part of me kept wondering how my mom was doing.

She'd had her minor operation on Friday. So I didn't get to talk to her all that day. And on Saturday whenever I called, Dad answered. He always said she was asleep, and that he'd call me when she woke up. But he never did call me. So I kept phoning the hospital. But I never did get to speak to my mom all that day.

After Buzzy and Fred and Red Sykes showed up, I didn't try calling any more. But I kept *thinking* about calling.

Anyhow, I knew my dad would be home around nine-thirty, because that's when he always gets home because visiting hours are over at nine. I could ask him then how Mom was.

Only he didn't get home at nine-thirty. At ten-thirty

he still wasn't home. Maybe he went over to see some friends or something. But at least he could have called!

Finally, around eleven o'clock I heard his key in the door and I ran downstairs.

Dad looked real pale. Like *he'd* had the minor operation.

"Where were you all this time?" I said.

He looked at me kind of surprised like he was wondering what I was doing there. Then he said, "Oh, hi, Robbie." And he blew on his hands. "Sure is a cold night out," he said.

"I didn't ask for any weather reports," I said. "Where were you all this time?"

He took off his overcoat. "At the hospital."

"But it's eleven o'clock now," I said. "Visiting hours are over at nine."

He hung his overcoat in the closet. "Yes," he said. "Well, on Saturday night they sometimes let you stay longer."

"Oh." I felt kind of relieved. "Well, at least you could have phoned me and let me know."

He didn't answer because just then there came this huge shriek from upstairs. We both ran up and into my room and there was Fred and Buzzy sitting on Red Sykes, pinning him down, and Buzzy was squirting my dad's shaving cream all over Red's face.

"What's going on here?" my dad shouted.

Fred and Buzzy jumped up like they were a jack-in-the-box.

Red got up too and started blowing the shaving cream out of his nose into his fingers.

"Just what do you think you're doing here?" my dad said. His voice was quieter now, but still very cross.

"They're sleeping over," I said real quick. "You said I could have some friends sleep over. It was Mom's idea," I added.

He nodded then. "Well"–he sort of waved at the mirror above my bureau–"I didn't say you could decorate the room." I saw then that while I was talking to my dad downstairs, someone had written Ha Ha and a couple of other words on my mirror with shaving cream from the aerosol can. It was the couple of other words I guess that got my dad angry.

Jud ran into the bathroom and came back with some wet toilet paper and started wiping off the mirror. He made a big smear but at least you couldn't read the words any more.

All that time no one said anything. We all just watched Jud in action.

Then my dad kind of nodded. "Well, try to keep the noise level down, boys," he said. "And lights off by midnight."

He walked out of the room.

I was surprised that he had suddenly got so nice. I wanted to follow him out of the room and ask some more about my mom and the operation. But I decided not to. Maybe he still was real mad and was just saving it up to be polite to my friends, but he'd turn it all on me when he got me alone. I decided to leave well enough alone and I didn't see him any more that night.

I did try to get the guys to "keep the sound level down," as Dad had put it. I explained that my dad was allergic to noise the way golden rod makes some people sneeze. The guys looked at me like I was a little strange. Or my dad was. But anyway, they kept kind of quiet. And we did put the lights out at twelve. I said that Red Sykes could sleep in my bed and I'd sleep in his sleeping bag which he'd brought over. I thought this might make up for him having shaving cream up his nose. But Red told me he didn't want to be separate from us, so we dragged my mattress onto the floor and we all slept in a line.

Not that we slept much. We talked a lot. When you're in the dark, things you say seem a lot more important.

Around four in the morning the others fell asleep.

I wanted to get up and go into my dad's room and ask him how the operation had gone. But I was scared that he'd be real angry at me if I woke him up.

So, I just lay there wondering.

9

After eight days I took my square chart out from under my pillow and tore it up. All the eight squares were filled in solid. But no one would say when my mom was coming home. So what was the use of keeping a chart?

Those days were really kind of terrible. I mean it seemed like nobody was telling me anything. Even my mom.

After that weekend I got to call her up again, like before. But it wasn't like before. She always sounded so tired. Her voice was the same. But it was like she was trying to *make* herself sound cheery. For me. She'd ask me about school and stuff, and I'd answer. I mean, if you wrote down the conversation it would read the same as before. But if you listened in, it wouldn't *sound* the same. For her, it was like an effort to talk and—what made it worse—it was like for the first time in our life she wasn't being quite straight with me. I mean, like I said, she'd always told me just the truth about things. If my mom said something, I could count on it: I could know it was so. But now—it wasn't that I thought she was lying to me. It was more that there were things she was trying not to talk about.

Like—she was having some kind of treatments. She didn't want to talk about *what* kind of treatments. Or why she was having them or anything. All she would say sometimes was that she'd just had a treatment and she was feeling kind of tired so could she call me back in a couple of hours.

As far as what I was saying to her, I wasn't too interested any more in telling her things like how Buzzy shot three straight baskets and we won the game. Or how I was getting more co-ordinated with my left arm since I still had to favor my right on account of the plates in it which weren't due to come out for another five months.

Sometimes what I really wanted to say would just shoot through all this nothing kind of talk. "Mom, I miss you so much!" I would say. Or, "Mom, when are you coming home?"

She'd tell me that she was coming home—soon. And she'd say, "I miss you too, Pumpkin." Sometimes she'd say these kind of things in her regular voice. But sometimes it was as though she was sort of crying.

In school, well, I guess I was really uptight. Very jumpy. It was like I was tensed up all the time and the littlest thing would set me off. I grew this really bad temper which I never had before. If someone started something with me—watch out!

It seemed like either I was very quiet, or I was getting into fights. Quiet, or yelling. Not much in between. Which is where I always used to be.

One time in the schoolyard a tenth-grader named Nick Something came up to me and said I'd hit his little brother with a drumstick. I said I didn't hit his damn brother or anybody ever with a drumstick. So this guy says I'm lying and punched me in the nose. I kind of exploded. Bad enough to be punched in the nose if you *did* hit somebody's kid brother with a drumstick. But if you *didn't!* I mean, I can't take it calm if I'm accused of something I didn't even do! This was one thing that always had set me off. And *now*—well, I just lit into that tenth-grader. Punched him as hard as I could in the face and in the belly and before I knew quite what was happening I had him down on the concrete and was pounding him, and guys from my class were standing around cheering me on like I was some world champ or something.

This Nick was screaming and blood was coming out of his nose and then Mr. Jenson came running over and hauled me off of him and wanted to know what was going on. (Only he didn't say it in such polite words.) I tried to tell him about the drumstick but I started to kind of cry and I ran across the schoolyard and into the building and locked myself in the bathroom. And then I did cry. But what was I crying about? Here I was a big hero beating up a tenth-grader and in my full rights to do so and I was crying in the john and trying not to let my sobs out—like it was me who had lost the fight.

When I got home from school that day I called up Mom and told her about the fight. I figured she'd be glad. She's very high on sticking up for what you believe in, so why shouldn't she be glad I'd stuck up for *myself* so good? But she sounded sort of far away. She said I shouldn't get into fights or it might slow my arm from healing. Then she said in her kind of joky voice, "Unless, of course, you're so co-ordinated now that you can beat up a tenth-grader with your left hand." She laughed a little. And I laughed a little too. Even though what she had said wasn't so exactly funny. I wanted to try to encourage her to make little jokes again, like she used to.

Maybe what made me the most worried during that time was my dad.

I mean he got really different.

Like I said, he never did talk too much to me at the best of times. But now he talked even less. It was even as though he was kind of avoiding me. Can you imagine *avoiding* your only child?

We got along all right. We didn't get into any arguments or anything. We were both sort of quiet.

He'd wake me up in the morning. Not cheery like Mom did. He'd just open the door at seven-thirty and say, "Time to get up, son. I'm leaving now. Have a good day."

And he'd take off.

Every day the same little waking-up speech. Like it was a part in a play that he had memorized.

I'd get my own breakfast, although, to be honest, I mostly went to school without breakfast. If Mom wasn't there to make my breakfast it didn't seem worth the bother to me to get anything for myself. Especially since I was hardly ever hungry. I guess my dad must have felt the same way. At least I never saw any of his dirty breakfast dishes in the sink.

By lunchtime my appetite took over. At first, like I said, I came home for lunch—mostly so I could phone my mom while I was eating. But as the weeks went by—yeah, I *did* say weeks!—she always seemed to be very sleepy around lunchtime. She'd tell me she was having a nap and could we talk later. And she did sound real weak and sleepy. So then I asked my dad if I could eat lunch in school and after school I'd hang around watching basketball practice or something. I mean what was the use of coming home with nobody there? My dad never got to the house until nine-thirty, when visiting hours at the hospital were over and then he'd just call up to me, "Hi, Robbie." And I'd call down to him, "Hi, Dad." Just like we used to.

Only it was all different.

He usually came home with a bag of groceries. Then he'd make himself some dinner. Sometimes I'd come down and fix dinner for him. I'm not too bad a cook. I learned from watching my mom cook things. But it didn't seem to matter to him what he ate. In fact, whatever was on his plate, he didn't eat much of it anyway.

I once asked him why he didn't eat his dinner at the hospital cafeteria. Then he or me wouldn't have to bother cooking and washing the dishes and pots and things. He said he didn't want to waste visiting hour time eating. He wanted to be with my mom.

He really did love her a lot. I was glad about that.

Maybe it was that he was loving her so much when she was there in the hospital, that he didn't have much love inside him left over for me.

It was sort of like we were two separate strangers living there in the house. Without my mom the place seemed pretty empty; pretty dead.

10

There are two kinds of terrible.

The first is regular-terrible. It can happen to anyone. Any time. Like me breaking my right arm at the beginning of the summer vacation. I mean, that is pretty terrible. You keep thinking, *Why did it have to happen to me!* And you gripe a lot. To yourself—if not out loud. I mean people would get real turned off if you complained around out loud. And that'd make the terrible even worse.

But the thing about this first kind of terrible is—well, it has an end. Not only you know it's the kind of thing that can happen to anyone any time. But you know it'll be over with one day.

Then there's this other kind of terrible—which makes the first kind shrink into nothing at all. The second kind has no end. And it's so much worse that there hasn't been any word invented for it. At least, no word that I know.

Things kept falling more and more into *that* kind of terrible.

My dad kept acting more and more depressed. Sometimes I'd look at him and his eyes would be all watery. And I'd look away. I knew he didn't want me to see him like that.

And my mom—well, one day I just couldn't help it. We were talking on the phone—and suddenly just out of nothing I said, "Well, when are you going to get all better and come on home?"

My mom started to cry. And then she said in a kind of smothered, teary voice, "I have to hang up now." And she hung up.

I mean, that really made my day great.

But that was nothing—compared to what happened the next night.

When my dad got home he didn't call up, "Hi, Robbie," like usual. Instead, he called, "Robbie, you want to come down here for a minute?" (He has this polite way of asking me to do things. *Do you want to*—but it doesn't mean that you can answer, *No I don't want to.*)

In fact, I *didn't* want to go down there for a minute. I don't know why, but I felt real scared.

When I went down my dad was sitting in his leather chair by the fire. It's the kind of chair that tilts back if you want to relax. Only there wasn't any fire lit, and he wasn't tilted back in his chair. He was sitting straight up.

"Hi, Dad," I said, "what is it?"

I was in my pajamas already, even though it was only nine-thirty. (In the last few weeks I'd been getting very good about going to bed and taking a bath and all that. At first when my mom went to the hospital I kind of liked having the freedom to go to bed when I wanted and to never take a bath and to eat all the junk food I wanted. But after a while the idea came to me that maybe if I did all the things I was supposed to do just like Mom would tell me to do if she was home, then it would somehow help to bring her home sooner. It was sort of a secret pact I had with someone, God maybe.

Anyway, I was in my pajamas, and I'd just had a hot bath and the living room where Dad sat in his leather chair was kind of cold. I started shivering.

"Are you cold?" Dad said.

"A little."

"Well, go up and get your bathrobe and slippers," Dad said.

So I went upstairs to put on my bathrobe and slippers. I kind of wondered why he couldn't come up with me and tell me whatever he had to say with me warm in my bed.

Anyway, when I came back down he was still sitting in the same stiff way in his leather armchair.

"Sit down, Robbie," he said.

There was another chair by the fireplace. But it was Mom's chair. She always sat there when she read or knitted or whatever. Especially on Sunday afternoons while Dad was reading his paper.

I didn't want to sit in Mom's chair, so I sat on the couch which is real comfortable. But I didn't lean back or anything. I sat on the edge. And I sat just straight. Like Dad was.

I was scared. And even though I had on my bathrobe and slippers, I still was shivering a little. At least, I was shivering inside.

Then my father told me. He talked very quietly. "Your mother has cancer," he said.

I nodded. As a matter of fact I had thought of that word a lot during the past weeks since she went into the hospital. In school . . . when I was doing my homework . . . especially in bed at night the word would suddenly take on a shape like a gruesome-looking monster and it would be there staring at me. The best way I had of making the word go away was telling myself that my mom had always been straight with me, and if that was what she had–she would have told me so. Or at least she would have told my dad to tell me. Since nobody told me, I could go on thinking that it was something else.

"Will she get better?"

"Well," my dad said, "where there's life there's hope."

Then he started telling me about all the things they were doing to make her better. Chemotherapy treatments and drugs and other stuff. I kept nodding like I was taking it all in. But I had sort of stopped listening. I felt like we were two characters in one of those cancer commercials you see on TV.

"Does Mom know?" I asked him.

"No one has told her," my dad said. "But–I think she knows."

"Yeah," I said. "She always has a pretty good perception about things."

It didn't feel like *me* sitting there talking about *my* mom. It was this boy on the commercial *acting* scared.

And then, suddenly, you know what happened, my *dad* started crying! I mean, he just sat there stiff upright in his chair and he was making these strange sobby sounds and tears kept running out of his eyes. He didn't even seem ashamed or anything.

It wasn't like any cancer commercial any more. It was us two. My dad and me. Alone. And it was terrible.

I got up and went to him and sort of half sat on the arm of his leather chair and I tried to put my arm around his back and he sort of turned to me like he was the kid and I was the father. He had his head against my bathrobe. I didn't know if I should wipe his tears or what.

"Is she going to die?" I said.

"The doctor said she had a twenty-five per cent chance," my dad said, but I could hardly make out the words because his voice sounded all sort of water-logged.

"A twenty-five per cent chance to die?" I said.

My dad took the end of my bathrobe belt and he wiped his eyes. "The doctor said she has a twenty-five per cent chance–to live. She has a very virulent type of cancer."

Then my dad stood up. And he was back himself again.

I wasn't myself, though. I was still someone else. I had to be. I had to not believe that it was my mom he was talking about. I had to believe that I was not me.

11

A few days later I said to my dad, "Can't I go visit her?"

I'd been saying that right along, even though the answer was always the same: *no visitors under sixteen.* I knew the answer like you know a phrase from a broken record that keeps sounding over and over till you shove the needle to a different place in the song.

Now it was as if someone *had* shoved the needle to a different place, because when I asked the question, my dad said, "Yeah. We'll try to arrange it."

Then I got really scared. How come I could see her now, when I couldn't before? Did they make exceptions when someone was almost—? When someone—?

In school that day, I was like numb. I didn't listen to what one single teacher was saying. My dad told me that he had called up the principal and had a talk with him about my mom and me at school and all. I guess the principal must have told my teachers because no one called on me or anything. Mr. Jenson acted real nice to me after class. He said, "How's it going, Rob?"

I said, "Okay."

He sort of rumpled my hair and said, "Good boy," like he was talking to a dog or something. But it somehow made me feel a little better.

Jud and I walked home together after school.

I hadn't said anything much about my mom, not even to Jud.

He'd ask me every so often how she was doing, and I'd say, "Okay, I guess." And that was about it. Maybe part of being a best friend is knowing when the other one doesn't want to talk about something.

But now I did want to talk.

I said, "I'm going to see my mom in the hospital tonight."

"Hey, that's great," Jud said.

"What's so great?" I said. "They don't allow any kids to visit if they're under sixteen. Not in the grown-up wards."

"Oh," Jud said.

"Do you think that means my mom is gonna die?" I said.

"What do you mean, *die?*" Jud said. His voice kind of squeaked.

"Well—why else would they suddenly let me visit her?" I said.

"Don't be *crazy!*" Jud said. "People's mothers don't

just—die like that. I never even heard of anybody whose mother died!"

"I didn't either," I said.

"Probably—your dad's got some pull at the hospital. Or maybe your mother's doctor has. And they're making an exception in your case.

"You think so?" I said.

"Sure!" Jud said in a very strong voice.

We were passing a stationery store where they sell newspapers and magazines and greeting cards and things. And Jud said, "You got any money on you?"

"What for?" I said.

"Well, you could buy your mother a present. When you go to see someone sick in the hospital you're supposed to bring them a present."

"Yeah," I said. "My mom brought me a lot of presents when I was in the hospital with my arm."

"Yeah," Jud said. "Remember that neat invisible ink set? Whatever happened to it?"

"I used it all up," I said.

"Can't you send in for more of the ink and stuff?" Jud asked.

"I guess so," I said. "I'll look on the box and see where to send off to."

"Yeah," Jud said. "Do that. We can play CIA agents."

I was glad to be talking about invisible ink instead of my mom and we stood outside the shop for a while, making up a CIA game.

Then we went inside. I only had a dollar and you sure can't get much for a dollar these days. I finally picked out this funny little fuzzy thing on a spring. You pull the string and it bounces up and down.

"Could you wrap it as a gift?" I said to the shop lady.

But she told me they only wrapped gift items that cost five dollars or more. Maybe I looked disappointed or something because she tore off a piece of gift-wrap paper and gave it to me. "There," she said. "Wrap it yourself, son."

Jud and I went home and we looked around for some Scotch tape to stick the gift wrap closed. Jud said he'd go over to his house to get some. But I said, "No! Don't! We don't need Scotch tape!"

Jud looked at me. Then he nodded. He knew I was asking him please to stick around until my dad came to drive me to the hospital. When you have a best friend, they know what you're saying even if you're saying something else with your words. Maybe not all best friends are like that. But Jud is.

When my dad drove up and honked in the driveway, Jud walked me out to the car and just before I got in he said, "Good luck, Robbie."

He knew that it wasn't because of pull that I was getting to see my mother in the hospital.

It didn't matter about the Scotch tape. She could hardly even open the package without it. That's how weak she was. She could hardly even put her arms around me.

Dad said she was all doped up with sedatives for the pain.

She looked terrible.

Her hair was kind of grayish. It used to be blond. And it always was clean. She was never one of these beauty-parlor types. She just had her hair simple; parted on the side, straight to her shoulders, and clean. She washed her hair a lot. Now it was oily-looking and grayish.

And her face was so thin. She never used to wear make-up around the house. When she went to a party with Dad, or if they had people in, she would put on lipstick and eye shadow and stuff. But at home it was just her regular face showing. And either way she looked good. But now her skin sort of matched her hair; grayish-looking.

I guess someone's eyes can't change. I mean, eyes are eyes; they can't get bigger or littler. But my mom's eyes looked bigger now, in her thin face; and they seemed so sad. Even when she smiled up at me, her eyes were so sad.

I didn't know what to say to her. So I didn't say anything. In fact, I couldn't say anything.

How could my mom change so much in such a short time?

I opened the present and showed her how this little fuzzy animal or whatever it was would jounce up and down when you pulled the string.

She smiled watching it. She liked it a lot.

"It's got a little spring inside it," I told her. "That's how it works.

She nodded. Then she looked at my dad and sort of moved her head toward the door.

Dad said, "I'll wait outside, Robbie." He went to the door and then he said, "Mom's tired, so—don't stay with her too long."

"Okay," I said.

When he had gone, Mom and I just looked at each other. There was so much I wanted to say to her. But right then I couldn't think of anything. I just looked at her. Then I asked, "Do you like what I brought you?"

She nodded, and she sort of motioned me to come closer. I sat on the bed. She tried again to put her arms around me but she couldn't lift her arms that high. I mean, she was so weak. I bent right over close to her and kind of helped her to put her arms around me. She was trying to tell me something. I put my ear right close to her mouth. She said, in such a soft voice, "I love you so much."

"I love you so much too, Mom," I said. I kissed her on the forehead.

Then she kind of gasped like she was in pain. I was real scared. "Do you want me to get Dad?" I said.

She nodded.

I ran out into the hall and Dad was there talking to some doctor. "Mom wants you," I said. "I think something hurts her." And they went quick into the room and suddenly I was there on the outside, waiting.

I don't know how long I stood in that hospital hallway. Visitors were going in and out of other rooms. Some people carried flowers and plants and wrapped-up book-shaped presents. The door opposite where I was standing was open and I could see inside this room where there were so many cards taped onto the wall that it looked like some kind of patchwork-quilt wallpaper. I guess they were get-well cards. I wondered if my mother had gotten a lot of those kind of cards. I wondered if she knew that she was dying.

After a while the doctor came out of my mom's room and told me that she had a kind of tummy ache and they'd given her something for the pain and she'd soon fall asleep. He said that my dad was staying with her, but would it be okay with me if he got the nurse to call me a cab so I could go home?

"I don't want to go home," I said. "I want to stay here till she wakes up."

"Well," the doctor said, "I don't know quite when that will be. I think it would be better if you go on home, son."

"WELL," I shouted, "I AM NOT GOING HOME!"

People passing in the hall looked at me. A nurse came over and asked if she could be of any help. "Wait here with him," the doctor said to her. Then he went back into my mom's room.

Pretty soon my dad came out and said, "Come on, son, she's sleeping. We'll go on home."

"Can I see her again?" I asked. "Can I see her sleeping?"

"Not just now," my dad said. "You can come back tomorrow. She'll probably be feeling better by then."

So we walked together down the hospital hall and we waited for the elevator, and we rode down to the parking lot level and we got out of the elevator and my dad gave a blue ticket to the parking lot man who brought out the car and my dad and I got into the car and we drove out of the hospital area and all of that without saying a single word to each other.

When we hit the main road out of town I looked at my dad and in the flash of light from a street lamp I saw the tears running down his face. Then he pulled the car way over to the side of the road. I guess it's not too safe to drive when you're crying.

"She's going to die, isn't she, Dad?" I said.

"When there's life there's hope," my dad said. Always when he'd told me that before, I believed it. But I didn't believe it any more.

My dad put his arm around me, and sitting there in the car, we cried together.

Crying together brought us closer together than we had ever been before in our lives. At least, I felt that way. I don't know if he did. And never before in my life did I need so much to be close to my dad as right then.

12

The next day I didn't get to see my mom after all. Because of my Aunt Emily, from Muncie, Indiana.

My dad had told me a couple of weeks ago that she was coming. *To look after things till your mother gets home.* That's the way he'd put it. I didn't know my Aunt Emily, because Muncie, Indiana, is a long way from us and there never seemed to be enough reason for us to visit her, or vice versa. So we never got together except my dad sent her snapshots of me every once in a while. And she'd write back to say how I was sprouting up and getting to look more and more like him every day. Personally, I don't think I look one bit like him. But he's not bad-looking at all, so at least she wasn't insulting me by saying it.

Anyway, when he told me she was coming, I was

glad to hear it because, if you want to know, the house had turned into one big mess with just my dad and me living in it. Mrs. Pandorus, the cleaning woman, came every Monday, like usual. But the Monday-house-cleanness sure didn't last long! I mean, it was easy to see all the things my mom had done in the house—when those things weren't done by my dad and me. We washed the dishes, and that was about it.

One Saturday I got ambitious and made my bed. Then I made Dad's bed. It was hard for me to do that because I hated to be in the same room where my mom's bed was—all neat and unslept in. But when I'd finished Dad's bed the room looked more the way it used to with both the twin beds made and waiting to be slept in.

When Dad got home from the hospital he didn't say thanks or anything about me making his bed. He didn't even seem to notice. So I figured the hell with it, and I never bothered making his bed again.

But my Aunt Emily would do all that, my dad said.

So when I came in the house and saw her there, I was kind of pleased. She's my dad's older sister, but she looks the opposite of him. He's on the thin good-posture side. And she's sort of plump and she has these fat legs and the beginning of a double chin. And my dad, as I said, has a kind of standoffish way about him. But his sister is the opposite: friendly.

As soon as I walked in she kind of descended on me and enfolded me in this big hug. I mean, after all, even though she's my aunt, she also was a total stranger. You feel a little uneasy being hugged by a perfect stranger.

Anyway, she kept me busy showing her where everything was in the house. The linen closet. Where we keep the Brillo. How the washer and dryer work. All that stuff. And then at six when I thought my dad would come from the station and drive me to the hospital to see my mom, Aunt Emily insists that we don't have a thing to eat in the house and she wanted me to show her where the supermarket was. I mean, she *could* have driven into town and asked someone where the supermarket was. In fact, I even told her that. And I told her I was planning to see my mom that evening. But she told me that Dad had phoned and said that Mom had been given some heavy sedative and she'd be sleeping all night so there wasn't any point in him taking me to see her tonight. Instead, he'd go straight to the hospital from the station, like usual.

"Well, if *he* can see her, why can't I?" I said to Aunt Emily. "I don't care if she's sleeping or what. I just want to see her, and they told me I could. The doctor said that yesterday."

"Honey," my Aunt Emily said, "I'm only following orders. Maybe if she wakes up tonight, I can drive you over to see her."

"You promise?" I said.

And she nodded. "If the doctor says it's all right. I promise."

So I went with her to the supermarket.

They have a pay phone, and I called the hospital. I figured my Aunt Emily could drive me by there on our way back. But when they rang my mom's room, nothing happened. The hospital operator said that the phone in that room had been disconnected temporarily and could she take a message. It had happened like that often before. "Just tell her that her son called," I said, and I hung up.

I felt like my insides were flaming mad. Why couldn't I sit there and watch her sleep like my dad was doing? I can understand how in the regular way they wouldn't want kids in the hospital. They might make too much noise running around and they could bring in germs; chicken pox and things. But my mom wasn't in the regular way any more. Shouldn't a son have as much right as a husband?

I didn't feel like talking on the way home. My Aunt Emily tried to make little chitchats but I guess she saw that I had my mind on other things. Finally, she took one hand from the steering wheel and put it on my knee and just pressed my knee for a second. It was sort of like when Mr. Jenson messed my hair in that friendly way. Sometimes a little thing like that can speak a lot more than a pile of words.

The rest of that night I was just one big worry.

I don't know which was the most terrible: the days or the nights. It kind of evened out. All the time I was filled up with this worry. In the day I'd have to try to hide it from my friends. But in the night in bed I'd be all alone.

Having Aunt Emily in the house didn't make the worry any less. And it didn't make the aloneness any less either. But at least that night I had the first good dinner since Mom went to the hospital. Rare roast beef and baked potatoes. Aunt Emily had asked me what my favorite meal was and that's what she made me. But I didn't feel too hungry. In fact, the dinner reminded me of a prisoner getting his choice of menu before he goes to the electric chair.

The next day–it was a Thursday–I came home after school and I walked in the door and there in the living room was my Aunt Emily—and my dad. They were both standing up. It was like they were waiting for me to get home.

Right away I knew. I could see it on their faces.

I said, "Oh, my God, no."

They both just stood there, looking at me.

Then my Aunt Emily came and started enfolding me in her fat arms. I shoved her away.

I walked into the living room and sat in my dad's leather chair by the fireplace. And I just sort of started screaming. I was like hysterical almost. I was like crazy.

My dad came into the living room and he stood there watching me. He was like one of those dummies in the department store window. Life-size. Stiff. Just standing there.

My Aunt Emily went into the kitchen.

I looked up at my dad and I screamed at him, "Why did she die? Why did you let her die?"

But he only stared at me.

I stood up and ran out of the room and up the stairs and into my own room and all the time I was screaming.

Finally, my dad and Aunt Emily came in. My dad sat down beside me on the bed. "Please, Robbie," he said. "Please son, take it easy."

My Aunt Emily said, "Robbie, dear, sit up, please. I've made you some nice hot chicken soup."

My dad said he didn't think I wanted any chicken soup. He sort of lifted me or pulled me up and I jerked away from him. I only wanted to be alone. Alone with my mom.

I ran into her room and threw myself on her bed and hugged her pillow like it was my mom and I kept on yelling and screaming.

They left me alone then. I guess they didn't know what else to do with me.

And I didn't know what else to do.

I'll skip all the rest of what happened that night. It was too terrible even to remember about. Mostly all that happened was crying. Me crying. My dad crying. Even my Aunt Emily crying, and she hardly knew my mom. It wasn't the together kind of crying like when him and me was sitting in the front seat of the car that night. It was the all-alone kind of crying. For me. And for him. Like you know you're going to be all alone for all the rest of your life.

The next morning my dad thought that it would be best for me if I went to school. So I went to school.

My dad had written a note which I gave to Mr. Jenson. The note said: *Please be kind to Robert. His mother died yesterday.*

13

The news got around quick.

It was terrible.

The kids were all whispering together. They didn't know what to say to me or how to act to me. It was like I had suddenly turned into some kind of freak or something. No one in the class had ever had a mother that died. And no one had told them how they should act. So naturally they didn't know.

A few of the kids came up to me and said they were sorry to hear what had happened about my mom.

I sort of mumbled, "Thanks." I mean what are you supposed to say? I guess no one wrote an etiquette book on *that* yet. It really hurt me when people asked me about her. Yet, on the other hand I was glad they did. At least it showed that these few kids were trying to make a bridge through to me so I wouldn't just be all alone surrounded by this whole sea of the most terrible sadness anybody could ever know.

I guess my dad was right to send me to school. I mean, if you go about your day's schedule the way you normally would, well, it helps a little. Once you're *doing* something your mind can kind of get off it a little. If you think about it all the time you could get crazy.

I thought maybe Mr. Jenson would help me. When the others went down for recess I sort of hung around a little. I was hoping he would tell me to stay behind and have a talk. He was at his desk, marking papers, and he looked up and said, "Robbie, I'm so very sorry."

"Yeah," I said. I was waiting for him to ask me to sit down and have a talk. I guess I was really waiting for him to tell me how to act and what to do.

But all he said was, "When is the funeral?"

I told him I didn't know.

Then he said I should call him up and tell him when it was and where because he'd like to come. "I knew your mother a little," he said. "I met her when she came in to do volunteer work at the school library. She seemed like a wonderful woman."

"Yeah," I said. "She is."

Then Mr. Jenson looked at me like he was thinking of what else he should say. And I looked at him, waiting for him to say it.

Finally, he smiled a little in a friendly way. "If I can do anything to help," he said, "just let me know."

"Sure," I said. "I will. Thanks." And I walked out of the room.

I guess he really did want to help me. Only he didn't know how.

Jud was the only one in the whole world who knew how. He kept on acting just like he had before. Not like I was suddenly some kind of freak; different because my mom had died. He didn't talk all mishy-moshy the way the few other kids did who talked to me about it at all. And he understood how I hated it the way the other kids were all sort of whispering and talking. Behind my back. Only I could see them and hear them. Jud knew how terrible that was.

He knew that I wanted some attention; not *Hey, I'm special. My mother died*. But attention of the companionship kind.

I don't know how I would have got through it without Jud. I would have been too all-alone to stand it.

I mean my dad sure wasn't any help.

The closeness that we'd had in the car that crying night all disappeared. It was like my dad who had always been uptight and into-himself, grew a whole new outside shell.

When we got home that afternoon, me and Jud—who had walked me home—my dad said to me, "The minister's here," and he said to Jud, "I think you'd better go on home, son."

Jud shrugged one shoulder and he said, "Sure, Mr. Farley." And he looked at me and shrugged the other shoulder.

Well, I guess my dad was in his rights asking Jud to leave. This business with the minister was supposed to be a real close family matter. Only we weren't a real close family.

The minister sat in my mom's armchair by the fire. I guess my Aunt Emily must have made the fire to have things a little more cheerful. The minister asked us questions about my mom. Her personality and her hobbies and all. I told how she liked gardening and how she loved animals. (We don't have a dog or anything, because my dad doesn't like pets in the house. But I didn't say that part. She would have liked to have a dog though. Along with me. I wondered suddenly sitting there whether my mom had wanted another kid, after me. And my dad had said no. It would have been better having some brother or sister to feel things with right now.)

The minister wrote notes down in a little black spiral book. In the middle his ballpoint pen got all scratchy because it had run out of ink and I had to go find him another pen. When I came back I told him how my mom used to wake me up so cheerful in the morning, and tuck me in every night. But he didn't write that down even though I'd just brought him this brand-new pen.

He didn't stay too long. When he stood up to go, he patted me on the head and said, "See you tomorrow,

Robert." It so happens that I hate being patted on the head. But I guess that's what ministers do. It wouldn't seem suitable maybe for them to muss your hair, like Mr. Jenson had done.

I phoned Mr. Jenson and told him that the funeral would be the next day and I gave him the name of the funeral home. That's where we had to go that night. To the funeral home. We just sat there, the three of us; my Aunt Emily and my dad and me. And at the other end of the room there was this huge coffin. I didn't even know if my mom was in there or not. And I didn't want to ask.

I didn't want anything—except not to be there.

That was one of the times they had better invent a new word for. A word which means a whole lot more than terrible.

The only way I could get through it was to pretend that *I* had turned into a department-store-window dummy. Or a kind of boy robot that could nod and say "Thank you" and stuff like that, but who didn't have any feelings at all inside.

These people come in and sign in the funeral parlor register book. And then they walk over and say things to you about your wonderful mother and you don't know what to say back except, "Yes, she was," and "I appreciate your coming." That's what my dad kept telling them. "I appreciate your coming." So I said it too.

Jud was there. And he stood beside me most of the

time. That was the only help I had. We didn't talk too much except to make comments under our breath. Like once he said, "I wonder how come all these oldies are showing up? *They* sure weren't your mother's friends." I told him it must give them a charge to come to funerals and see someone else lying in the coffin instead of them.

I found myself introducing Jud a lot. Since he was standing right beside me, people would say to me, "And who is *this* young man? And I'd say back, "This is Tom Judson, my best friend." Sometimes I wouldn't even say his name, I'd just answer: "This is my best friend."

It made me feel a little better—letting people know that I had a best friend who wanted to come and stand by me even in a funeral parlor. I mean, a lot of kids' best friends would have stayed at home watching TV or something on this Friday night.

After people had "paid their respects" (that's how my dad put it) they would stand around in little groups and talk about how they hadn't seen so and so since whoses wedding and did you hear that Agnes had a baby girl. I mean, it seems to me very rude to gossip around about nothing when somebody's mother and somebody's wife is lying at the other end of the room in a coffin.

The whole thing was so terrible that I didn't even cry. And neither did my dad. I was like frozen inside. Maybe he felt that way too. But I guess we were supposed to cry because there was this box of tissues on a table right by where we were sitting. I took the box and put it underneath my chair. They sure think of everything at the funeral homes. I wondered whether they'd put it on the bill: *Tissues, 1 box.*

The next morning this huge black Cadillac picked us up to take us back to the funeral home. I don't know why we couldn't have driven there in our own car like we did the night before. But I guess these funeral homes got their own way of doing things—ways that are going to make them the biggest pile of money.

I'd asked my dad whether Jud could come along with us in the limousine. But he said no. It wouldn't be appropriate. It was just for The Family.

"Yeah," I said in a sour voice. "The Family! Sure."

What—*family?*

14

So there we were—the three of us—this great Family—sitting in a huge Cadillac that would have held twenty people.

I felt like a real weirdo. I was all dressed up in a tie and white shirt and my best suit (my only suit, if you want to know). Except the trousers were a little short. High waters we call them in our school when your legs have grown too long for your pants, and it's like you've pulled them up to wade through water. Anyway, there wasn't time to buy me new trousers.

When we were driving along Elm, which is one of the main streets in town, I hunched down real low because I sure didn't want to be seen by anyone I knew. Any kids, I mean. What you *don't* want is the way everyone right away considers you so—different when your mother dies. So, naturally, if one of your friends sees you sitting there in this huge car they're going to think you're more different than ever. Sort of freaky.

This time we were ushered into a different hall in the funeral home. A chapel, sort of. And this old man in a uniform leads us down to the front row of seats and unhooks this long cord of stuffed velvet and we sit down. If you didn't care about the one who died maybe you'd feel like a celebrity or something, with all this special attention and reserved front-row seats, and everyone sort of looking at you. But there was the coffin up on the stage underneath all these flowers. And that was mostly what I was thinking about. I couldn't believe that my mom was in there.

I figured I wasn't supposed to look around too much, so I just gave a couple of glances back. First the seats were all pretty empty and I felt insulted for my mom. I mean, I knew she had all these friends. So—where were they? Out shopping at the supermarket? Or playing golf or something on this nice, sunny Saturday morning?

I saw Mr. Jenson sitting there, right beside Jud. They both sort of waved at me, and I gave them a kind of smile back. Did you ever feel like you were somebody else? That's how I felt then. I didn't feel sad, or mad, or anything much. I was just—observing. It was as though they had attached one of those intravenous things to my arm. Only instead of feeding glucose into me, like in the hospital, it had drained all the feeling *out* of me. I was kind of glad I felt that way. I mean—who wants to sit there crying in front of a bunch of strangers?

The funeral was called for eleven and by that time the place had filled up pretty much, and right on the dot the minister started. (He'd told my dad that another party had reserved the chapel for eleven-thirty, so we'd all have to be out by eleven twenty-five.)

Listening to this minister I began to get some feeling back. Not feeling of sadness. Feeling of madness. Here he'd gone to all the trouble to come to our house and copy down notes about my mom in his little spiral notebook. But the speech he was giving had nothing whatever to do with *my* mom. It could have been anybody. He kept mentioning her name, Susan. But nobody ever calls her Susan. My dad calls her Sukie. And her friends call her Susie or Sue. Or even Sooz. Susan is—somebody else.

That's who he was talking about. Somebody else. Anybody else. Nobody else. It was some set speech he'd made up so he wouldn't have to bother himself saying something different about each separate person who dies. Maybe he's got three speeches. One for a lady. One for a man. One for a child. And he sticks in the dead person's formal name. And that's it. He doesn't have to trouble himself any more.

Mostly he talked a lot about God.

Maybe that's a help to some people. I guess it is—if they're a really religious type. But my family never has been too religious. As a matter of fact, the minister talking on about God and his wisdom made me kind of glad I didn't believe so exactly much about God and heaven and all. I mean I guess it can be good, having someone there night and day to tell all your troubles to. Though it always struck me as kind of conceited to think that God has time to listen to you just at the moment you want to tell him something special, when there are all these other millions of people in the world who might be needing to talk to him at the exact same minute. But maybe being omnipotent and omnipresent and all these other omnis makes it possible for God to talk to millions of people in all parts of the world at once. Or at least to listen to them all at once. For their sake, I hope so. But for my own sake, right then the minister was making me more and more glad that I wasn't too depending on my belief in God. Because if I had believed a lot, well right then I would have been so angry at God that I think I would have stopped believing. God in his wisdom, the minister kept saying. I mean, what kind of wisdom is that–taking a perfectly good human being like my mom, someone who had never done any harm to anyone so far as I know–and killing her with cancer (which, my dad told me, spread to her liver and that's how come she died so quick). I mean, I need my mom. And dad needs her. But what does God need her for? Who's he trying to punish? Me? For what? What'd I ever do to him—except not to believe in him too much. But is that any reason to kill my mom? And my dad's a perfectly good man. I mean, he works hard to support his family. I'm sure he does everything a good man is supposed to do; and I'm sure he doesn't do any of the bad things that it says in the ten commandments thou shalt not.

I mean, so he's kind of a cold fish. That's no crime. Anyway, I don't think he was that way with my mom. He loved her too much.

Maybe the best thing about being religious is, you can talk things over with your servant-of-god. Your minister or priest or rabbi, or whatever. Maybe if I'd been going to church and had some minister more along the lines of Mr. Jenson, then he could have been a help to me now.

But this minister—whose name was Dr. Randolph—I don't think he'd have been of much help to anyone even if they'd started being religious way back in the first grade of Sunday school. I wondered where my dad had gotten him from. Maybe he was hired by the funeral parlor. Part of the whole package.

After the service was over, we had to drive out to the cemetery. Again I asked my dad if Jud could ride in our limousine. Again, he said it wouldn't be proper. (I mean, if something makes you feel better why shouldn't *that* be what's proper? Anyway, I didn't say any more about it. My dad at least seemed to know what to do. Which is more than I did.)

I sat by the window which is always my favorite seat in a car. I like to open the window wide and let the air rush in. Even though it was winter, it was a warm day. Maybe Mom would have gone out to play golf today. Anyway, the fresh air felt good. But my Aunt

Emily told me to close the window because the wind made her cold. So I closed it. I was wondering how this fattish stranger in the black dress could be sitting beside me in the car, and not my best friend Jud. Then I wondered how come she had the black dress, all so appropriate. Did she know my mom was going to die when she took the plane from Muncie, Indiana? Had she come all fitted out for the occasion? She even had this little black lacy thing which she fastened to her hair with bobby pins. Right then I hated my Aunt Emily, but I don't really know why. After all, she was trying her best to be nice. And she probably would have a lot rathered to stay with her own family in Muncie.

As for my dad, during that whole drive he just sat staring out his window. Maybe he felt like I did, that he was somebody else so he didn't have to feel anything about any of this at all. On the other hand, maybe he was feeling things. Every once in a while he sort of sniffled—but more like someone who's coming down with a cold than someone riding out to a cemetery behind the coffin of his wife.

I was kind of hoping my dad would say something—memorable. About my mother; or how we would have to make it together without her. Something that would help. But he didn't say anything at all. Not one single word. Maybe if I'd been sitting next to him, he would have put his hand on my knee, the way Aunt Emily did that day in the car coming back from the supermarket. But we were separated by her and by all the other space between us, so he couldn't touch me even if he wanted to.

The cemetery was like a gray stone forest of petrified tree stumps. Each gravestone stood for someone dead; each gravestone stood for the same kind of terrible sadness and loneliness I felt. I wondered how many kids had been out to this place because their mother or father died. Thinking about these other kids made me feel a little comforted somehow. I wasn't the only one. I mean, with all those hundreds of gravestones, there must have been at least a few standing over some mother or father who had a kid my age.

Some of the dead people must have been really rich. They had these little marble houses with pillars and everything built right over their graves.

We had to walk quite a way till we got to the place where my mom was going to be put.

Then, suddenly, there it was. The long, deep hole in the ground. The coffin was in it already. And this Dr. Randolph was there waiting. I wondered how he'd got into place so quick. Half of the hole was covered by planks with artificial grass on them.

The wind started blowing up cold.

My dad stood next to me. Then he put his arm around my shoulders. Because he felt like it? Or because he felt that he should? I wondered, but I didn't know.

I looked around. All I could see was all the people who didn't come. I mean, it wasn't that far from the funeral parlor to this graveyard. And everyone has cars. Why didn't they come? Well, I know it's no big pleasure to stand by somebody's grave. Maybe it would remind them that it could happen to them too—just as quick. And no one wants to think about that. And who can blame them.

I only half heard Dr. Randolph when he started talking about dust unto dust. I mean, I'd seen this same scene in the movies. That's how I felt. Like I was watching some movie. Not even like I was *in* the movie. Unless a kind of extra or something.

I felt that way until—I heard the sound.

Dr. Randolph took up a handful of dirt and he dropped it down and I heard the dirt hit onto my mom's coffin.

That sound did it. The little soft clunks of dirt dropping onto her coffin. Suddenly I knew. Like a terrible scream coming out of the sky. It was my mom down there in that box. A few days ago she had put her arms around me and she had whispered, "I love you so much." And now she was down there in that box and I couldn't ever reach her again.

I turned and ran, stumbling against gravestones that I could hardly see because I was crying so much. I didn't know where I was going. I just wanted to get away from that place where my mom was being buried under dirt and wooden planks and artificial grass.

I heard my dad calling after me, "Robbie, wait!"

But I just kept running on.

15

When we got back from the cemetery it was kind of crazy. Our cleaning woman, Mrs. Pandorus, had shown up while we were at the funeral. And when we got home, there she was all decked out in a starched white uniform, standing behind our dining room table. And on the table was a whole bunch of mixes and dips and potato chips and little triangle sandwiches with the crusts cut off.

She started showing my Aunt Emily all she had accomplished that morning. And then the doorbell rang and these people who had been at the funeral parlor and others who hadn't even showed up there came swarming into the house like we were having some New Year's Eve party or something.

I didn't know what to do. I wanted only one thing—to be all by myself. I didn't even want to see Jud. Not then. And suddenly there were all these people clumping in. Some of them brought cheese and bread and cake and stuff as though having my mom die meant we would be starving.

My dad had told me that a few people might drop around in the afternoon. But he didn't warn me about any party!

Mrs. Pandorus gave me a big tray with a Camembert cheese on it and some little round slices of bread. And she told me to go around to the people and offer the cheese. I asked her why they couldn't get their own cheese and she said it was more polite to pass it. Especially, she said, since we had Camembert cheese, imported from France, we might as well show it off special. It was very expensive, she said, and she told me not to offer any to the same person twice. Mrs. Pandorus seemed all charged up being a party manager all of a sudden. She didn't say a word about my mom. All she said was, "How was the funeral?" I said, "Fine." And then she gave me instructions about how I should slice the Camembert cheese.

So there I was at the most terrible time of my whole life, walking around like a zombie serving out cheese to a bunch of gabbing people. All I wished was that they'd get the hell out and go home.

But when they did finally clear out and go home—you know what? I wished they were back again!

Why? Because then came the most terrible time of all. Mrs. Pandorus washed up the dishes and left around eleven that night. My dad went to bed. I don't know how he could even go into that room where my mom had slept right there in the made-up twin bed. On the other hand, there wasn't any place else for him to sleep, since my Aunt Emily was sleeping on the sofa bed in the sewing room—which got called the guest room if a guest ever stayed overnight, which hardly ever happened.

Anyway, they went to bed around midnight.

I did too.

And then, lying there in the dark, I suddenly knew. It was like my bed was a coffin and my room was a huge cavern, a grave. And I was at the bottom of it.

I wasn't dead. But I was being buried. By aloneness.

My mom wasn't ever coming back home. It was the kind of terrible that had no end. Ever.

Now I would be living in this house with my dad, who was a stranger.

That was what I suddenly knew as I lay in the dark on the funeral night. My dad was a stranger. I was terrified.

I didn't know how I could live on without my mom. Maybe she and me had been too close. Me being the only child, and her not working except sometimes as a volunteer in the school library. She had always been there. I had no practice in living without her, except the last eight weeks when she was in the hospital. But then at least I could talk to her on the telephone sometimes. Now there wouldn't be any answer ever again. Last year in English we studied this poem, by Poe. "Quoth the raven, 'Nevermore.'" Maybe that's the scariest word there is: *Nevermore.*

Or, maybe the scariest word is *alone;* at least for a kid. I guess everybody needs somebody. But a kid needs somebody even more. And I had nobody. I had a father who was a stranger.

Maybe it's hard to see how that could be when we were living in the same house—him and me—ever since I was born.

As a matter of fact when my mom was alive I never did think of my dad as being a stranger. He was my father and I loved him and I knew that he loved me and if he had some lacks in him as a dad—well, so do a lot of fathers I know. (Buzzy's father drinks too much, just for example.) Anyway, any lacks *my* dad had—well, my mom filled in for him just fine, so I didn't notice them hardly.

But now, lying there in the coffin-dark, it hit me. I might say it exploded in me. Without my mom, what *was* there between my dad and me? What had there ever been?

Who *was* this man who used to come home every night and call up to me, "Hi, Robbie," and I'd call down, "Hi, Dad"? Even my mom never talked much to me about my dad.

Suddenly I realized that on weekdays when my mom was alive I sometimes wouldn't even *see* my dad from one day to the next! He was gone when I got up in the morning, and often when he got home at night I'd be in the middle of a good TV program or I'd be doing my homework, and then it'd be my bedtime, so what would be the point of going all the way down to say "Hi, Dad," or "I'm going to bed now"? So I'd just get in bed.

I guess with the combination of his cold-fishy sort of personality, and his not liking kids or pets too much, and his commuting every Monday through Friday to the city, that's what it added up to: a man who was a stranger to his son.

How would we ever get on together alone in the house?

I found out the answer soon enough. The answer was: we got along terrible.

The next morning my Aunt Emily had to leave.

It's weird. As soon as someone's been to the funeral and "paid their respects" by bringing cheese or whatever to the house, then they seem to think they've done their duty and they wash their hands of the whole thing.

It was that way with my Aunt Emily. I mean I really wanted her to stay around for a while. A few days at least. So what if I hardly knew her? So what if I had some down opinions about her in the car riding out to the graveyard? I still didn't want her to go *home!*

Just by making dinner and mopping the kitchen floor and holding me in her arms and kissing me and things like that, she was—helpful. You know? And her being there held off the time when I'd have to be all alone in the house with my dad.

But when I asked that morning if she couldn't postpone her flight home, she looked at me a little surprised. "Sweetheart," she said, "I'd love to stay. But I have my own family in Muncie. I'm afraid I have to get back."

So I nodded as though I understood, even though I didn't.

It's not as if I had a great horde of other relatives I could turn to—or run away to, if it came to that. You see my mom and her folks came over from England when my mom was three years old. And when my mom was in college, her parents and their other kids went back to England and stayed there. So I've got this set of relatives across the ocean. But I've never even met any of them. We Christmas-card each other. And that's about it. Although my mom and her folks write letters back and forth every once in a while. (Excuse me, if I talk about her sometimes like she's still alive. It's hard not to. She was so much alive when she *was* alive, that to me she still very much is. And it helps me sometimes thinking of her as *is*, not *was*.)

Anyway, my dad's family is very small. Just him and his older sister Emily and their mother who I only saw twice in my life. She's got this bad arthritis, so she can't get out of the house much. And somehow we never got around to visiting her in Muncie, Indiana.

So there it was, my one good relative, Aunt Emily. And she was leaving on the morning plane.

I sort of hung around in the guest room while she

packed her suitcase. Then she took a newspaper article out of a side pocket in her suitcase and she said, "I cut this out for you, Robbie, I thought it might help a little." She handed it to me.

"Thanks," I said. The headline on the article was: HOW TO HELP A CHILD TALK OUT HIS FEELINGS AFTER A PARENT HAS DIED.

The date the article had been printed was—two weeks ago! Did Aunt Emily know two weeks ago that my mom would die?

I asked her.

"Well, yes," she said. "Your father phoned me and told me the doctor had said—" She broke off.

She didn't need to say any more. When my dad kept telling me *Where there's life there's hope*, he knew it was a lie. There wasn't any hope. But maybe it hadn't been all a lie. Maybe *he* still had some hope. Privately. Maybe he had to.

"Robbie, dear," my Aunt Emily said, "is there—I mean, as the article says, is there anything you'd like to talk about? Any—questions you'd like to ask?"

"No," I said. Then I said, "Yes!"

She sat down on the bed, and waited.

She had to wait awhile because it was a hard question for me to ask.

Finally, I got it out. It was a question I couldn't ask my dad. But I needed to know the answer. "Before she went into the hospital—"

My Aunt Emily waited some more.

"Well," I said, "I'd hear them arguing downstairs. They never used to argue before. They always loved each other a lot."

"And you want to know if your dad ever told me what they were arguing about?"

I nodded.

My Aunt Emily stood up. She enfolded me in her arms. "Yes, pet, I know." She sighed: I heard it, and I felt it, since she was pressing me tight against her front. "Your mother was having these pains. I guess she'd been having them for some time–before your dad was even aware of it. But you know, she had this–thing against doctors. For herself anyway."

"Yeah," I said. I moved away from out of her arms. (I don't know why. I kind of liked being enfolded.)

"Well," said my Aunt Emily, "that's what the arguing was about. When your dad found out about her pains, he insisted she go for a checkup. And she insisted there was nothing wrong with her. She said she'd wait for her regular checkup time."

"And who won the fight?" I asked.

"Your dad did. Finally."

"But–finally was too late."

"Yes," my Aunt Emily said, "I guess your mother was afraid to go. Afraid to find out. Maybe that's what it was."

"If she'd have gone earlier, when the pains began?"

This time my Aunt Emily didn't answer. Maybe she couldn't. She went back to packing her suitcase.

Suddenly, like a lightning flash, I hated my mom. If she'd gone earlier, when the pains began, maybe she wouldn't have had to die and leave me all alone.

16

When my Aunt Emily left, it was just like I knew it would be. Except worse.

I stopped hating my mom. I had to. There has to be somebody you love and feel close to, even though they're dead. Sometimes I'd still go all cold with hating her for not having her checkup on time and dying. So what if you hate going to the doctor? If you're a hermit in a cave with no relatives and got only yourself to worry about, okay then, it's your life and your death and your choice. But I guess even a hermit may have some pet deer or raccoon or something that comes to him to be fed. I mean, if there's other people or pets counting on you to keep alive —then you have to be responsible to them, don't you? And if you go to all the trouble to have a child, then it should be like a contract with yourself. You've got to take care of yourself for your kid. So what if you don't like doctors! Big deal! Go anyway!

I wanted to talk about this with my dad. I wondered if he hated her too sometimes, for the same reason. That article my Aunt Emily gave me was right. It would have been a help to talk things out. But there's one little necessary item required: someone to talk things out *to*.

Jud was some help. But you can't tell a kid your own age that sometimes you hate your dead mother. I mean it just wouldn't sound–appropriate.

I couldn't talk to Mr. Jenson. We just weren't that far along in our relationship. Also, in school I was my other self.

It was like I grew this shell. It looked just the way I had looked before my mom died. When I wore this shell I could act the way I had before my mom died. And I wore it every day to school; like putting on my clothes. With it on I was maybe even better in school than I'd been before. Not that I was some boy genius before. But I always did pretty well in school. Now I concentrated even harder, and did my homework even better. I found that if I got on with my life it helped me to stop thinking about my mom's death.

The kids in school seemed–relieved that I was the same as before. (At least *they* thought I was the same.) That meant they didn't have to treat me any different–the way they had the first day my mom died. I just went along as though nothing had happened. And so did they.

Only once in a while something came up in school

that I wasn't prepared for and my shell split apart. Like once we had this substitute teacher in science. I was fooling around with the test tubes and Bunsen burners and laughing with Buzzy, who was my partner. And finally this substitute science teacher got very cross and she said real loud, "Robert, if you don't get on with your experiment, I'm going to call your mother and tell her how you've been acting up."

Well, there was this real dead silence. Everybody in the class knew—except the substitute science teacher.

"Yeah, do that," I said then. "Call my mother!" And I rushed out of the classroom, because I had started to cry.

At home I always took my shell off. I mean my dad wasn't trying any too hard to make things easier for me. So I figured why should I bother pretending in front of him?

We weren't together in our sorrow, the way it had been that once in the car when he pulled over to the side of the road.

Now our sorrow kept us even more apart than we'd been before.

Once my dad told me, "Robbie, if you ever have to talk to somebody—I'm open."

What a weird way to put it. I'm open. Maybe he read that article Aunt Emily left me. Anyway, I didn't take him up on his offer. I mean, you can't talk over deep feelings like that with someone you hardly know. So I was sort of stuck on my own.

As for my dad, well, it was as though he took out his sorrow on me. Maybe he didn't mean to, but that's how it was. He'd explode in madness over these little things he never even mentioned when Mom was alive. Like if I left my towel on the bathroom floor after a shower. Sure I should have picked it up or put it in the hamper. But so what if I forgot? Is that something to start shouting about? I mean, when Mom was alive I guess she used to pick up after me. I was kind of spoiled in that way. I didn't have any chores or anything. Well, after all, she was there in the house all day with nothing much to do, so why should she leave over some chores for me? At least that's how she must have figured it.

Anyway, here I was with no chore-training, and suddenly I had all this stuff to do like putting clothes in the washer-dryer, and folding them up and sticking them in the right bureau drawers, and putting a pot roast in the oven (Dad liked getting one big hunk of meat that we could eat cold after the first time) and carrying out the trash on Tuesday and Friday mornings, which is when they collect it around here. And washing the dishes, which is one thing that I happen to hate. Well, you'd think Dad would give me a little gratitude at least for the things I *was* doing—instead of sounding off on the things I forgot to do.

Sometimes he'd apologize for hollering at me. Like once when I asked him why we couldn't hire Mrs. Pandorus to come in a couple of times a week instead of just on Mondays.

My dad shouted out real loud: "*Because we can't afford it! That's why!*"

I just stared at him. I mean, what's to shout about so much? Why couldn't he just say it in a normal voice?

I guess my stare got to him. Anyway, after a minute he said, very soft, "Forgive me, son. You asked a perfectly reasonable question. The answer is: I owe a lot of money. Hospital bills. We'll have to cut down expenses. Not add to them."

I nodded.

Then I went out into the kitchen. He hadn't eaten dinner yet. I had. But I found myself setting the kitchen table with two plates; two of everything. I don't even quite know why.

He came into the kitchen, and he said, "You waited to eat with me?" He sounded pleased.

I gave him a sort of smile.

Then I got out the cold roast beef and sliced some off with the electric knife and I made some salad and we sat down, opposite each other.

"Looks good," my dad said.

"Yeah," I said. I stuffed a hunk of roast beef in my mouth so I wouldn't have to talk. Frankly, I didn't know what to say.

"I guess we shouldn't be splurging on roast beef," my dad said, "when we're so broke. On the other hand, we save on all the extras. Soup, vegetables and all that."

"Yeah," I said. My dad doesn't go in for this nutrition business at dinnertime, like my mom used to. He considers a well-balanced meal is something he likes to eat. Maybe he was thinking about my mom too, and her nutrition because he suddenly said, "Did you take your vitamins this morning?"

"Vitamins?" I hadn't taken a vitamin since the day Mom went into the hospital.

"You've got to keep up your vitamins," my dad said, kind of sternly. "You're still a growing boy." Then he smiled a little. "I guess I have to try to take over where your mother left off."

"That's okay, Dad," I said.

"I've got to try to be a mother and a father to you now."

I looked at him. *Never mind you being a mother*, I wanted to tell him. *Just try being a little better of a father. That'll be good enough.*

To encourage him in this, the next night I really did wait with my dinner till he came home. What's more, I had the table all set in the dining room—where he and Mom used to eat together.

"You want a drink Dad?" I said after he took off his overcoat.

"Sure, son," he said. "I'll fix it. Why don't you have a Coke or something with me?"

He sat in his armchair sipping whatever it was that he made for himself. And me, I sat in Mom's chair.

He said, "Well, how was school today, Robbie?"

I said, "Fine,"

He said, "Well, what'd you *do?*"

I said, "Work."

It went on like that. We were not exactly relating to each other relaxingly, you know?

If my mom had asked me the same questions I would have found plenty to say.

Then he went on inquiring into each of my separate classes. What were we learning in math? How much homework did I have in science? Would I show him my English composition? It wasn't like he really cared. It was like he had read the article and was following instructions on what they said to do.

Anyway, I felt it was good that he was coming out of his sorrow enough to ask about my life, whether he really cared or not.

That night the house didn't seem quite as empty.

And that night when I went to bed—I didn't want to tell this part—it makes me sound like too big a baby. But anyway—every night since I knew that my mom was going to die, I cried when I got to bed. No one knew it because I put the pillow over my head and cried against the sheet.

I cried on this night too. But I didn't feel quite so much that my loneliness was choking me. I felt that there was some kind of hope for me and my dad together. For a long time I lay in bed, staring up into the dark. Then, without even thinking about what I was doing, or why, I got up. I put on my slippers so he wouldn't yell at me for walking around barefoot on the cold floors. I put on my bathrobe. And I went into his room.

I wanted to know if he was choking with loneliness in the night like me. I wanted to ask him if he would like me to sleep in his room, in the twin bed.

I thought that maybe if we two were together in the dark, sometimes we might be able to talk out inside things. After all, maybe he needed to talk as much as I did. Especially to talk about my mom. Because we had hardly said a word about her since she died.

Very softly I opened the door to his room.

17

The TV was on. And my dad was sitting in the armchair, watching it. The room was dark except for the sort of faded glow from the TV screen, and the bright spot of his cigarette. Was this what he did in the night for company, watched old movies till 2 A.M.?

He seemed very involved. He didn't look up when I walked in.

Then I saw why. He was asleep. Asleep holding a lit cigarette!

"DAD!" I shouted out. "Are you CRAZY?"

He jumped up like I had shot him. When he jumped, some heavy book fell off his lap onto the floor.

"DO YOU WANT TO BURN THE HOUSE DOWN?" I shouted. "We got enough of nothing as it is. Do you want us to have no HOUSE, for Christ sake?

What the hell are you doing, sleeping there with a lit cigarette?"

"Goddammit, don't you talk to me like that!" He took three long strides. He was next to me; tall over me. And he slapped me hard in the face.

I punched him with all my strength in the stomach.

Then I ran out of the room.

I locked the door of my own room. I got into the bed and pulled the blankets up over me, and held the pillow on my head. Not because I was crying. I wasn't. You don't cry when you're solid anger inside. Anger and hate. I hated him.

Like I said before, if there's one thing that gets me flaming mad it's being accused of something I didn't do. He was *wrong*, falling asleep with a lit cigarette. He *could* have started a fire. They've got this green shag rug in there. It could catch fire like a dry field of grass.

So what does he do? Instead of apologizing to me, he hauls off and hits me in the face. He never hit me in his life before.

Sure, maybe I was wrong to hit him back. I know I was wrong. I never even heard of a kid that punched his own father in the belly. But I was so mad I didn't know what I was doing.

Later on I heard him knocking at my door. But I just held the pillow tighter over my head like it would protect me. And I didn't answer.

I thought I was too angry to fall asleep. But I must

have slept because after a while it was morning, and I heard him knocking again at the door.

"Open up, son," he said. "Unlock this door, Robbie."

But I didn't answer. I listened though. I listened to hear if he was going to call some apology through the door.

But all he said, after a long pause, was, "Okay. If that's how you want it." And he walked away. I heard his footsteps fading off down the hall.

When he had left the house I got up. I didn't have breakfast. I went to school. I didn't even try to concentrate on anything. I was too much filled with anger to think about Julius Caesar or how to make possessive plurals or any of the other stuff we were studying. One time Mr. Jenson called on me. I didn't even hear him. The first I noticed was when different kids were looking at me, waiting.

"What?" I said to Mr. Jenson.

He repeated the question. Maybe I would have known the answer if I had thought about it. But I couldn't think. When you have too much emotion in you, your normal thinking can't get through. "I don't know," I said.

Mr. Jenson nodded and asked somebody else the question, and I went back to my brooding.

I guess Mr. Jenson knew that something bad had happened. Jud knew too. After school he said, "Come on and watch basketball practice, Robbie."

But I didn't want to. I wouldn't be able to play until the plates were out of my arm. And I sure didn't want to sit watching other guys having a good time doing what I would like to be doing. And I couldn't ask Jud to come on home with me because he's on the basketball team. He plays center. That's what I used to play before I broke my arm.

So I went home alone.

I walked into the house and it was like wall-to-wall emptiness.

I went up to my room. I switched on the radio: this rock station I used to like. Somehow I hadn't tuned it in since my mom went to the hospital. I don't know why.

Also, I hadn't played my drum since then.

But now I suddenly wanted to play. I needed to play.

I dragged my desk chair over and sat in front of the snare drum. And I started beating on the skin like crazy. I'd stop. Listen to the drummer on the radio. Then I'd fly off on my own. Improvise. I didn't only hit my drum. I'd slash out on my radiator. The bedpost. The wastepaper basket. It sounded great. I was making my own music.

I needed more. More sounds. I went downstairs and got the dinner bell my mom used to ring when Sunday dinner was ready. I tied it to the bedpost and there was another great sound.

I don't know how long I sat there. Beating it out. Improvising. Making music. It must have been hours because suddenly my dad was knocking hard at my door, which still was locked.

I guess he must have been knocking for a while, but I didn't hear anything through the loud rock on the radio and the sound of my drumming.

"Have you had your dinner, Robbie?" he called out.

"Yeah," I called back.

I hadn't. But I didn't want to see him. The drumming had gotten some of the anger out of me. But not enough. I knew if I went out I'd have to apologize for socking him in the stomach. I know that's not appropriate for a kid to do. On the other hand, he had no reason to haul off and hit me. So what if I swore at him? I had plenty of right to swear. If I hadn't gone into his room when I did, he *might* have burned the house down.

Anyway, I knew I wasn't going to apologize unless he did first. And I sure knew he wasn't going to do any apologizing to me! He never has once done that in his whole life.

He took hold of the doorknob and rattled on it. "Come on, Robbie," he said. "Open up. Don't be stupid."

I picked up my drumsticks and started making music again. Loud!

The next morning I ate a huge breakfast. My dad had left, so I could eat in peace. And I hadn't had any dinner the night before so I was famished. I made myself pancakes, bacon, the works. I was practically late for school because of eating so much.

Maybe the good breakfast made me feel better. My mom always told me it worked like that. Anyway, by the time I got home that afternoon, I decided to try to make things up with my dad. After all, he was all the family I had in the world, so I might as well try to make the best of it.

By way of easing back, I straightened up the living room some. I made my bed—which usually never got made except on Mondays when Mrs. Pandorus came and changed the sheets. Then I decided to make my dad's bed. That would show him as soon as he walked into the bedroom that I was silently saying I was sorry. Maybe I wouldn't even have to put it into words.

I took off the blankets and the top sheet, and threw the pillow onto my mom's bed. And guess what! Underneath his pillow there was a photograph album.

We have quite a lot of albums downstairs with the record collection. All the others have bright covers, calico and plaid; like that. And they have pages with sticky stuff on them. You just put the pictures under the cellophane, and they stay in place.

But this album under my dad's pillow was different. It was big and thick and black. Black cover. Black pages. And most of the pictures were black and white, stuck in with little gray corner tabs. This was what my mom called her old-fashioned album. It had a few pictures of her as a baby, and as a kid in school. (She was kind of plain; too skinny.) And as a girl in college. (Better-looking then.) But mostly it was pictures of my mom and dad in the early days of their marriage.

I'd looked through this album a couple of times, a couple of years ago.

But now I sat down on the bed and I really looked at it. Slowly. Page after page.

Page after page of their life together before I was born.

HONEYMOON. My mom had written the word in white ink at the top of one page. There she was smiling, with his arm around her. She looked beautiful. Like a living smile. And he looked—great. No wonder she married him! His hair was thick and wavy. Not like now. He was real handsome.

There were pictures of them on the golf course. And playing tennis. I'd forgotten this picture of them playing tennis. My mom had never told me that she could play tennis. Were they just posing for this picture with tennis rackets? Or did they really play?

I realized there was a lot I never knew about their early life before I was born. As a matter of fact, there was hardly anything much I *did* know about that time.

I kept turning slowly through the album; pages headed OUR FIRST APARTMENT . . . LAKE PLACID SUMMER . . . VISIT TO MUNCIE, INDIANA . . . ENGLISH SUMMER . . . and then . . . ROBBIE ARRIVES. Me in a baby carriage . . . my mom holding me up toward the camera, me stark naked . . . my mom holding me as I slept and her looking down at me with this sweet smile.

Suddenly I realized that this was the book Dad had on his lap that night when I found him asleep by the TV.

And the fact that he had it under his pillow . . . maybe he looked at this book every night before he went to sleep.

Then I had what might be the most important shot of understanding in my life.

18

Like I said before, it was terrible for me that my mom had died. But I suddenly knew that however terrible it was for me, it was even worse for my dad.

After all, most of *my* memories of her were from the last few years. I hardly even *had* many memories of her that reached back to the time I was three and four years old. And no memories before that—that I can remember.

But my dad had almost twenty years of memories they made together. *Two decades!*

Also, I had all these things ahead of me. Getting married . . . honeymoon . . . first apartment . . . having a kid. But my dad, well, he had lost his lifetime mate.

I felt so sorry to think of him sitting there night after night, alone; looking through the memories in this photograph album. I felt so sorry for him that all my anger at him went away.

But I didn't quite know what to do about it. Or what to do about the photograph album. Finally, I took the pad and pencil that's always kept beside the telephone and I wrote a couple of sentences. Really I should say that the sentences wrote themselves, because I didn't even know that they were in my head until I read them on the telephone pad.

> Dear Dad: I made your bed
> because I love you and we're all each other
> has and we should try to make things better
> for each other and not worse.
> Your son, Robbie

I didn't know where to put the note. Or whether I should put the photograph album back under his pillow. Somehow it seemed wrong to me to put it there. He had hidden it; so he must have been ashamed of it, sort of. He'd be still more ashamed—if he knew that I knew.

Okay, so I'd show him he didn't *need* to feel ashamed.

I made the bed as nice as I could. I even made smooth hospital corners, the way Miss Solomon had done when I was in the hospital. I put on the bedspread, and I put the album right on top of the pillow and fastened my note to the album cover with a paper clip.

But something still seemed wrong. It was like I was telling him that in my view it was great for him to be sitting every night looking at these old memories.

Then another sentence came in my head. I wrote it at the bottom of my note.

P.S. Another thing I was thinking, Dad.
There's no use putting the past in front of you.

I felt kind of nervous waiting for him to come home. I was trying to concentrate on my science report on pollution. When I heard his key in the lock my heart started to go faster. I had left the door of my room wide open so he could see right away that I didn't want to lock him out any more.

He called up to me, "Hi, Robbie," just like he used to. In the same friendly voice. (I guess he'd been doing some thinking during the day too. And some forgiving.)

I called back, "Hi, Dad!" Was he going to come up? Would he first go into his room and read my note?

I didn't know what to do, so I just kept on trying to write my pollution report.

I heard him coming on up the stairs.

He came into my room. "Hi, son," he said.

"Hi," I said. I stopped writing and looked at him.

"Homework?" he said.

"Yeah."

"You had your dinner yet?" he said.

"Not yet."

"How about noodles and clam sauce tonight?"

"Sure," I said.

"It's cheaper than roast beef anyway," my Dad said.

"I'll make it," I told him. Last time he tried noodles they came out all stuck together and sort of mealy-tasting.

"Good," he said. "You're a better noodle-maker than I am." Then he added, "You're pretty good on the drums too."

"Thanks," I said.

He reached over and tinkled the dinner bell that I'd tied to my bedpost. "No wonder it sounded like a whole band going in here when I got home last night."

"That was mostly the radio you heard," I told him. "I was just banging along."

"Well"–my dad stood up–"I don't know much about rock or drums but it sounded to me like you were doing more than just banging along."

Then we went downstairs together.

It's funny how you can apologize to each other when you're talking about noodles and clam sauce. I mean all the time making dinner together and eating it together and sitting together in the living room after dinner, him reading the newspaper and me doing my pollution report on the dining room table, all those hours neither one of us said a single word about being sorry that we'd hit each other. But all that night we both of us *were* saying that we were sorry. It was the best night I had ever spent with my dad. It was the closest we had ever been, except in the car that time when we were crying. And you can't depend on those kinds of terrible times to bring you close.

On this night it was just–regular closeness. Or, a beginning of closeness.

I read him my pollution report, as far as I'd gone.

He said it was damn good. And then he gave me a few suggestions, and I said they were damn good. And we even laughed.

About ten o'clock, I went up to bed.

This night I didn't put the pillow over my head to hide the sound of my crying. As a matter of fact, this night I didn't even cry. I lay waiting, listening, for him to come upstairs and go into his room.

While I was waiting, I fell asleep.

In the morning, he knocked at my door, and said, "Time to get up, son. I'm leaving now."

"Okay," I said, through a yawn.

I figured he might come in and say something about the note I had left. But he didn't. I heard him going quickly down the stairs and out the door.

Maybe he wanted to say something to me, but he didn't know how. So he got out fast. Before he'd have to.

When I went downstairs I saw an envelope by the front door. It had my name on it. In his handwriting.

It was weird, I thought, as I took out the sheet of paper. Him *writing* to me. Why couldn't he say whatever it was? But, after all, it was me who had started it. I couldn't say it. I'd written to him.

His note said:

> Dear Robbie: Thank you for your love.
> And thank you for your wisdom. Your
> words have helped me very much.
>
> Dad

That night I waited for him to come.

I don't mean I waited in my room with my door open.

I mean I waited in the living room. I even looked out the window a couple of times.

I watched him park the car in the driveway. I don't know why I was waiting. I felt kind of embarrassed about it—since I never had ever done that before. Maybe I wanted to thank him for his note; only not in direct words. Maybe I wanted that he shouldn't have to come into a house that seemed so empty.

I went to the window again—and I saw the strangest sight! My dad was coming up the front steps carrying three huge, bulky black shapes. I thought they were laundry bags.

I opened the front door and he sort of staggered in. He put the black vinyl shapes on the floor. Without saying a word. I zipped them open. Then I let out a shriek. *Drums!*

A new bass drum. A beauty. With a pearl finish. A new snare drum. And a floor tom-tom.

"A set of drums!" I mean I never knew you could cry when you're happy—but my dad seemed all smeary through my tears.

"There's more," Dad said.

He went out to the car and came back with the rest. Cymbals. And two small tom-toms to be attached to the bass drum.

We sat on the floor together and put screws into the

stand and fastened on the cymbals. "You call this a hi hat," I said to my dad.

He laughed. "When the man in the shop told me you needed a hi hat, I thought he meant some kind of costume."

I laughed too. "But all these other things, Dad," I said, "how did you know what to get—just exactly what to get?"

He took a page out of his pocket. "I found this when I was going through your mother's things." It was a page torn from a music catalogue. Once long ago I had circled this set of drums with a red crayon. It was like putting a circle around a dream. But my mom had found it. She had saved it.

"I guess your mother was planning to get you this sometime," he said. "For your birthday. Or Christmas. But hearing you play the other night—well, I figured you were ready for this set right now."

"God, Dad!" I said, "I won't even be able to fit all this into my room."

"I thought of that," he said. "How about we'll turn the sewing room into a music room? A practice room, for you."

"God, Dad!" I said.

We carried everything upstairs and set it up in the sewing room. It just fitted good.

Then my dad sat down on the sofa bed.

I looked at him.

"Well, after I spent all that money," he said "at least I deserve a sample of how it sounds."

"Sure, Dad," I said. I took the chair from Mom's sewing table and set it down in front of my drums. Then I looked at him. "But Mom always told me not to practice when you were home. She said you were allergic to noise."

"To noise, maybe," my dad said. "Not to the music my son makes when he plays the drums."

So I sat down on my mom's sewing-machine chair, and I started to play. I whammed at the cymbals, I stamped on the foot pedal, and my two new drumsticks were going like crazy as I sounded out a wild new song.

PEGGY MANN, her husband, Bill Houlton, and their two daughters, Jennifer and Betsy, live in a brownstone in New York City. There are two other members of the family: Jake and Tutu, a small mutt and a large one. Jennifer Houlton plays the featured role of Greta Powers in the NBC-TV daytime serial, "The Doctors."

Peggy Mann's by-line has appeared in most of our national magazines, and she has written thirty books, some for young readers, some for adults. Her best-known book for adults is: *The Last Escape: The Launching of the Largest Secret Rescue Movement of All Time*. This book was a Literary Guild Alternate. Her most recent story for very young children is *King Laurence the Alarm Clock*.

Two of Peggy Mann's books for children have been dramatized as hour-long television specials: one was *My Dad Lives in a Downtown Hotel*, a story of divorce, which was nominated for an Emmy Award. The other was *The Street of the Flower Boxes*, which won a Peabody Award and became the inspiration for a nationwide beautification campaign.